Academy Mystery Novellas

Volume 4
GREAT BRITISH
DETECTIVES

Academy Mystery Novellas

Volume 4

GREAT BRITISH DETECTIVES

Edited by
Martin H. Greenberg & Edward D. Hoch

Published by The Reader's Digest Association, Inc.,
1991, through special arrangement with Academy
Chicago Publishers.

Library of Congress Cataloging-in-Publication Data
Great British detectives.
    (Academy mystery novellas; v.4)
    1. Detective and mystery stories, English.
I. Greenberg, Martin Harry. II. Hoch, Edward D.,
1930—   . III. Series.
PR1309.D4G66 1987 823'.0872'08 87-19375
ISBN 0-89733-266-0 (pbk.)

Academy Mystery Novellas are collections of long stories chosen on the basis of two criteria—(1) their excellence as mystery/suspense fiction and (2) their relative obscurity. This second criterion is due solely to the special limitations of the short novel/novella length—too short to be published alone as a novel, but too long to be easily anthologized or collected since they tend to take up too much space in a typical volume.

The series features long fiction by some of the best-known names in the crime fiction field, including such masters as Cornell Woolrich, Ed McBain, Georges Simenon, Donald E. Westlake, and many others. Each volume is organized around a type of crime story (locked room, police procedural) or theme (type of detective, humor).

We are proud to bring these excellent works of fiction to your attention, and hope that you will enjoy reading them as much as we enjoyed the process of selecting them for you.

Martin H. Greenberg
Edward D. Hoch

Contents

THE BEAUTY SPECIALIST
by Leslie Charteris

*Leslie Charteris was born in Singapore in 1907, the
son of an English mother and a prosperous Chinese
surgeon, Dr S. C. Yin. Educated in England after the
age of twelve, he sold his first story at sixteen and
published his first novel when he was only twenty. The first
Saint novel,* Meet the Tiger, *followed a year later when
Charteris had just turned twenty-one. It was to be the
first of some 150 novels, novellas and short stories about the
Saint, whose popularity in films, television series and even
comic strips continues to the present day.*

*"The Beauty Specialist" is one of the best of the
numerous Saint novellas that Charteris produced early in
his career, a thriller of the Edgar Wallace school. In a
sense the early Saint books helped to fill the void left by the
death of Wallace in 1932, though Charteris and the Saint
went on to far greater popularity, especially in the United
States. Here we find the Saint battling a master criminal
known only as the Z-Man, the sort of villain Wallace
would have loved. Charteris ceased writing the Saint
stories by the mid-1960s, but the series was continued for a
time by other writers under his supervision.*

"The Beauty Specialist" first appeared in the British
Thriller *magazine, March 27, 1937, under the title "The
'Z' Man," and was collected in June of that year under
its present title as one of three novellas in* The Ace of
Knaves.

I

The fact that Simon Templar had never heard of the
"Z-Man" was merely a tremendous proof that the Z-
Man himself, his victims and the police authorities had
joined forces in a monumental conspiracy of silence. For
the Saint invariably had a zephyr finger on the pulse of

the underworld, and the various forms of fun and frolic that went on in the ranks of the ungodly without his knowledge were so few that for all practical purposes they might have been regarded as nonexistent.

He was lunching alone at the Dorchester Grill when the first ripple of new adventure irrigated the dusty dryness of a particularly arid spell. He had been ruminating on the perfidious dullness of the cloudy day when the grillroom was suddenly supplied with its own sunshine. A girl had entered.

She was alone. She was tall and trim waisted and as graceful as a dancer, and the soft waves of her fair golden hair rippled in the gentle stir of air caused by her own motion. Exquisitely dressed, devastatingly sure of herself, she was escorted to a vacant table in a sudden hush of awed admiration that enveloped a world-famous film producer, two visiting bishops, three cosmopolitan millionaires, a music-hall comedian, a couple of ancient marquises and about fifty other minor celebrities, in a simultaneous speechlessness of homage. Simon Templar, who had as many human instincts as any of the aforesaid, would have stared at her anyway; but somehow he found himself watching her with even more than that natural curiosity and interest. And a faint tentative tingle went through him as he realized why.

For an instant, when he had first raised his eyes and seen her, he had wondered if Patricia Holm had missed an appointment of her own and had come to join him. This girl was surprisingly like Pat; the same height, the same fair grace, the same radiant charm. There was something vaguely familiar about her face too; and now the Saint was no longer reminded of Pat. He wondered who she was, and he was not the kind of man to be satisfied with wondering.

"Tell me, Alphonse," he murmured to the waiter

who was hovering about him like a ministering angel, "who is the vision in smoke blue at that table over there?"

The waiter looked across the room.

"That, sir," he said, with a certain visible contempt for such ignorance, "is Miss Beatrice Avery."

Simon wrinkled his brow.

"The name strikes a chord but fails to connect."

"Miss Avery is a film star, sir."

"So she is. I've seen photographs of her here and there."

"Her latest picture, *Love, the Swindler* is the best thing she's done," volunteered the waiter dreamily. "Have you seen it, sir?"

"Fortunately, no," answered the Saint, glancing with some pain at the waiter's enraptured face, and then averting his own. "Swindlers have never interested me— much."

The waiter departed, hurt, and Simon continued to watch the girl at the other table. It was only a transient interest which held him, his inevitable interest in any exceptionally beautiful girl, coupled with the additional fact, perhaps, that Beatrice Avery was certainly a great deal like Pat. . . . And then in an instant, as if an invisible magic wand had been waved, his interest became concrete and vital. He flipped out his cigarette case and put a smoke between his lips. Nobody could have guessed that his attention was more than casually attracted as he lighted his cigarette and inhaled deeply; the sudden lambent glint that came into his blue eyes was masked behind their lazy lids and the filmy curtain of smoke that trickled from his nostrils. But in that instant he knew with the blissful certainty of experience that the syncopated clarions of adventure had sounded in the room, even if no other ears were tuned to hear them.

As the girl had seated herself a waiter had deftly

removed the "reserved" card which had been conspicuously displayed on the table, and the cloud of obsequiously fluttering *chefs de restaurant, maîtres d'hôtel,* waiters, *commis* and miscellaneous bus boys had faded away. Evidently she had intimated that she was not yet ready to order. The girl had then given the grillroom a thoughtful once-over as she removed her gloves and lighted a cigarette. These trifling details Simon had noticed while his own waiter was burbling about *Love, the Swindler.* All very proper and correct—and commonplace. But that which followed was not commonplace at all. Beatrice Avery's cigarette suddenly dropped from her fingers to the floor, and the colour drained out of her face until the patches of rouge on her cheeks and bright-tinted lips stood out in vivid contrast to the deathly pallor of her skin. Her eyes grew wide and glazed with terror, and she stared at the table as though a snake had suddenly appeared through a hole in the snowy cloth.

Simon hadn't the remotest idea what it was all about. That was the common factor of most adventures—you usually didn't until you were well into them. The difference between the Saint and most other men was that most other men were satisfied to wonder and let it go at that; whereas the Saint had to find out. And Simon Templar had discovered after some years of experiment that the most direct way of finding anything out was to go and ask somebody who knew. Characteristically he didn't hesitate for a second. Almost without any conscious decision on his part his seventy-two inches of lean, debonair immaculacy had unfolded from their chair and were sauntering across to Beatrice Avery's table; and he was smiling down at her with sapphire lights twinkling in gay blue eyes that few women had ever been able to resist.

"Could you use an unemployed knight-errant?" he murmured.

The girl seemed to shrink back. Some of the colour had returned to her face, but her eyes were more terrified than ever. He could see at close quarters that her resemblance to Pat was purely superficial. She had none of that calm ethereal tranquillity that was Pat's very own. She opened her bag as if she was too dazed and desperate to have grasped what he was saying.

"I didn't expect you so soon," she said breathlessly.

He was a bit slow on the repartee for two reasons. First he was wondering why she had expected him at all; and secondly he was searching the square of snowy whiteness with its gleaming glass and silver for some explanation of the frozen horror that he had seen in her face. Everything was in order except for the fact that a knife and two forks were out of their correct places and laid in a peculiar zigzag. Even the most fastidious stickler for table ceremony would hardly have registered quite so much horror at that displacement of feeding tools, and Beatrice Avery looked like the healthily unceremonious kind of girl who wouldn't have cared a hoot if all the knives and forks and spoons were end up in a flowerpot in the middle of the table.

"I came over as soon as you sent out the distress signals," Simon began and then he stopped short out of sheer incredulous startlement.

The girl had taken something from her bag, and she was looking at him with such an expression that the words died a natural death on his lips. She had conquered her fear; and instead of the terror that had been there before her eyes were charged with so much loathing and hatred and disgust that Simon Templar knew just what it felt like to be one of those wriggly things with too many legs that make their abode under flat stones. The reaction was so amazing and unexpected that for once in his life the Saint was at a loss for words. He invariably had such a totally different effect on beauteous damsels in distress that his self-esteem felt as though it had been hit by a coal truck.

"I have nothing whatever to say to you." The girl suddenly thrust a bulky envelope into his hand and rose. "But if you have any regard at all for my feelings please return at once to your own table."

Her voice was low and musical, but it had in it the bitter chill of an arctic night. She didn't look at him again, or she would have seen the utter bewilderment in his eyes. She closed her red mouth very tightly and walked gracefully with a steady tread towards the exit. Simon was convinced that she had never done anything half so fine before the camera.

He stood and watched her out of sight and then returned slowly to his own table in a kind of seething fog. The manhattan he had ordered earlier had arrived, and he drank it quickly. He felt that he needed it. And then in a hazy quest for enlightenment he took another look at the envelope which she had left in his paralyzed hands. It was not sealed; and the numbed feeling in the pit of his stomach tightened as he glanced into it.

"Well, well, *well!*" he murmured softly.

His tanned face hardened into bronze lines of puzzled concentration, with his eyes steadied into fragments of blued steel against the sunburned background, for the envelope was stuffed full with Bank of England notes for one hundred pounds apiece.

He withdrew the ends and flicked his thumb over them. Without careful counting he calculated that the wad contained about a hundred bills—ten thousand genuine and indisputable pounds. After his recent experience and in spite of the manhattan he was in no condition to resist shocks of that kind. Boodle he had seen in his time, boodle in liberal quantities and many different forms, but he had always worked for it. He had never seen it come winging into his hands when he wasn't even looking for it, like pigeons going home to roost. At any other time he would have been inclined to accept it as one of the many inexplicable beneficences of his devoted guardian angel; but he didn't feel like that now.

He couldn't get that look of hers out of his mind. It hurt his pride that she could have mistaken him for the common and vulgar agent of some equally common and vulgar blackmailer. It seemed obvious enough that that was what had happened. . . . But was it? Simon didn't know exactly how many dazzling figures it took to write down Beatrice Avery's annual income, but he knew that film stars were burdened with hardly less colossal living expenses, for they have to scintillate off the screen as well as on or else risk submersion in the fathomless swamps of public forgetfulness. And the Saint doubted very much if Beatrice Avery, for all her fabulous salary, could afford to whack out ten thousand pounds as if it were chicken feed. A sum like that spoke for a grade of blackmail that could hardly be called common or vulgar: it hinted at something so dark and ugly that his imagination instinctively tried to turn away from it. He didn't like to believe that such a golden goddess could have anything in her past that she would pay so much to keep secret. It made him feel queerly grim and angry.

He finished his lunch, paid his bill and then looked up the name of Beatrice Avery in the telephone directory. Her address appeared as 21 Parkside Court, Marble Arch. Simon made a mental note of it, paid a call in Piccadilly and then strolled along to his own apartment in Cornwall House.

"Anybody called, Sam?" he inquired of the wooden-faced janitor; and Sam Outrell detected a faintly thoughtful note in the Saint's voice.

"Were you expecting somebody, sir?"

"I'm always expecting somebody. But this afternoon, in particular, I shall expect a lady, gloriously fair and graceful, with wavy golden hair—"

"I know, sir. You mean Miss Holm."

"No, I don't mean Miss Holm," said Simon as he strolled to the elevator. "The lady's name, Sam, is Miss Avery. If she appears before you with my name on her rosebud lips shoot her straight up."

He was whisked to his floor, and as he let himself into his apartment he found Hoppy Uniatz in the living room's best easy chair with his feet on the table. Mr Uniatz was chewing the ragged end of a cigar, and there was an expression on his battle-scarred face which indicated that all was right with the world. The empty whisky bottle on the table may have contributed its own modest quota to this happy state of affairs.

"Hi, boss," said Mr Uniatz cordially. "Where ya bin?"

Simon spun his hat across the room.

"Lunching at the Dorchester."

"I got no time for dem fancy places," said Mr Uniatz disparagingly. "Dose pansy dishes ain't nut'n to eat. Now yesterday I find a swell jernt where a guy can get a kosher hamboiger wit' fried onions an' all de fixin's—"

"I wondered why that cigar was so overpowering," said the Saint, moving carefully out of range of Mr Uniatz's breathing. "I'm not sure yet, Hoppy, but there are indications that fun and games hover in the middle distance."

"Who's dat, boss?" asked Mr Uniatz, struggling valiantly to get his grey matter flowing.

This was no small effort, for nature had only provided him with a very small quantity, and even this was of a gluelike consistency.

"You may be right about the Dorchester," said the Saint sourly as he eased himself into a chair. "Anyway, it didn't do me much good. A charming young lady gave me ten tousand quid and the dirtiest look of the century. Tell me, Hoppy; has anything happened to my face to make it look as if I'd blackmail charming young ladies?"

"You look okay to me, boss," said Mr Uniatz blankly. "Who is dis dame?"

Remembering Mr Uniatz's mental disadvantages, Simon told his story in simple one-syllable words that would have sent the director of children's hour programs delirious with delight. He had had so much practice in that difficult exercise that Mr Uniatz, in spite of the limitations of his cerebral system, finally grasped the basic facts.

"De goil t'inks you are some udder guy," he said brightly.

"You put it in a nutshell, Hoppy," said the Saint admiringly.

"De guy who puts de black on her."

"Precisely."

"De guy," persisted Hoppy, working nobly to get all his facts in order, "who is playing games in de distance."

The Saint sighed and was bracing himself to go into further laborious explanations when the sound of the telephone bell spared him the ordeal. He went to the instrument.

"Two visitors for you, sir, but they ain't ladies," said Sam Outrell hurriedly.

"Give me two guesses."

"You ain't got time for guessin', sir," interrupted the janitor. "It's Mr Teal, and he's lookin' madasell, and he went straight up without letting me call you first. He'll be there any minute—"

"Don't worry, Sam," said the Saint imperturbably. "I'm not leaving. Go out and get Mr Teal some chewing gum, and we'll have a party."

The doorbell rang violently, and Simon Templar hung up the telephone and went out to admit his favourite visitor. And the absolute truth is that he hadn't a cloud on his conscience or any suspicion that the visit would be more than a routine call.

II

Chief Inspector Claud Eustace Teal thrust his large regulation foot into the opening as soon as the Saint unlatched the door. It was an unnecessary precaution, for Simon flung the door wide and stood aside invitingly with a smile on his lips and the light of irrepressible amusement in his eyes.

"Come in, souls," he said genially. "Make yourselves at home. And what can I do for you today?"

The invitation was somewhat superfluous, for Mr Teal and the man with him, whom Simon recognized as Sergeant Barrow, were already in. They hadn't waited to be asked. They came in practically abreast, and Barrow kicked the door to with his foot. The Saint was compelled to back into the living room in face of that determined entry. There was an unusual aggressiveness about Mr Teal; his plump body seemed taller and broader; the phlegmatic dourness of his round pink face under its shabby derby was increased by the hard lines of his mouth. He looked like a man who was haunted by the memory of many such calls on this smiling young buccaneer—calls which had only lengthened the apparently hopeless duel which he had been waging for years against the most stupendous outlaw of his day. And yet he looked like a man who had a certain foreknowledge that this time he would emerge the victor; and a kind of creepy puzzlement wormed itself into the Saint's consciousness as the meaning of those symptoms forced itself upon him.

"Hi, Claud," said Mr Uniatz in friendly greeting.

Chief Inspector Teal ignored him.

"I want you, Templar," he said, turning his sleepy eyes on the Saint.

"Of course you do, Claud," said the Saint slowly. "Somebody has sold an onion after closing time, and you want me to track him down for you. A gang of lemonade smugglers who have eluded Scotland Yard for years have been—"

"I mean," Teal said immovably, "that I'm taking you into custody on a charge of—"

"Wait!" said the Saint tragically. "Think what you'd be losing if you really pulled me in. What would you do with your afternoons if you couldn't come round here for these charming little *conversazentes?*"

"All the talking in the world won't save you this time, Templar," said Mr Teal in a hard voice. "Do you want to see the warrants I've got? One for your arrest and another to search this flat."

The Saint shrugged watchfully.

"Well, Claud," he said resignedly, "if you want to make a fool of yourself again it's your funeral. What's the charge this time?"

"Demanding money with menaces," said the detective flatly. For a moment his eyes lost their sham of perpetual boredom; they looked oddly hurt and at the same time contemptuous. "You know how much I've wanted to get you, Templar; but now that the time's come I'd just as soon not have the job. I never thought I shouldn't even want to touch you."

Simon glanced down at his brown hands, and in his mind was a vivid memory of Beatrice Avery's look of unutterable loathing. Teal's voice contained that very look, transmuted into sound. His pulses, which up to that moment had been ticking over as steadily as clockwork, throbbed a shade faster.

"Is there something the matter with me?" he asked curiously. "Have I suddenly taken on a resemblance to Boris Karloff, or is it only a touch of leprosy?"

"You're the Z-Man," retorted Mr Teal and stopped chewing his cud of tasteless chicle.

There was a silence that pressed down on the four men like a tangible substance. It was as though the air had become a mass of ectoplasm. Hoppy Uniatz broke the suffocating spell by shuffling his feet. It is doubtful if more than a dozen words of the conversation had infiltrated through the bony mass which protected the spongelike organization of nerve endings which served him in lieu of a brain; but the impression was growing on him that Mr Teal was making himself unpleasant.

"What was dat crack again?" he said, his unmusical voice crashing into the silence like a bombshell.

"Yes, Claud," said the Saint gently. "What was it?"

"You heard me the first time," Teal said crunchily. "You're the Z-Man; and if I couldn't prove it I wouldn't have believed it myself. It's something new to know that you've sunk as low as that."

Simon moved across to the mantelpiece and leaned an elegant elbow on it. He pulled hard at his cigarette until the end glowed red; and the smoke stayed down in his lungs. A dim light was breaking in the darkness through which he had been groping his way: he saw in his mind's eye the disarranged knives and forks on Beatrice Avery's table in the Dorchester Grill, and he knew the meaning of that queer zigzag formation. They had shaped the letter *z*; and it was the sudden sight of this that had caused the girl's terror.

But the light was still not enough. . . . The Saint's eyes switched over to Mr Teal, and their clear blue glinted like the sheen of polar waters under the sun.

"My poor old blundering fathead," he said kindly. "I'm afraid you're off the rails again, for the umpteenth time. I don't know what the hell you're talking about."

"Dat goes for me, too, boss," contributed Mr Uniatz, who had clearly understood every word of the Saint's last terse sentence.

Mr Teal's lips thinned out.

"Oh, you don't know what the hell I'm talking about?" he barked. "Are you going to deny that you were in the Dorchester Grill an hour ago?"

"Why should I deny it? I lunched there."

"And you spoke to Miss Beatrice Avery?"

"We had a few brief words, yes. Of course I suppose that was very wicked of me, because we hadn't been introduced—"

"You took a package from her."

"No."

"You deny taking a package from her?" shouted Mr Teal.

"I do. She thrust the package into my hand and breezed off before I could even examine it—"

Teal's face turned a shade redder.

"You're not going to save yourself by quibbling like that," he snarled. "It's no good, Templar. You can try it on the jury. You're under arrest."

He took his right hand out of his pocket for the first time in that interview; and a pair of handcuffs clinked in it.

Simon glanced at them without moving.

"Hadn't you better think again, old dear?" he suggested quietly. "I don't know why I should go out of my way to save your hide, but I suppose I'm funny that way. Perhaps it's because life wouldn't be the same if you got chucked out of Scotland Yard on your ear and couldn't bring your tummy round to see me any more. Perhaps it's because I object to being marched into Piccadilly with bracelets over my wrists. But somehow or other I've got to save you from yourself."

"You don't have to worry—"

"But I do, Claud. I can't help it. It'd keep me awake at night, thinking of you sleeping out in the cold gutters with no one to even buy you a piece of spearmint. And it's all so obvious. The whole trouble is that you're jumping to too many conclusions. Just because I'm the Saint, and you never found any other criminals, you think I must be all of them. Then you hear of some guy called the Z-Man, so you think I must be him too. Well, who the hell is this Z-Man, and why haven't I heard of him before?"

Chief Inspector Teal bit on his gum in a super-charged effort of self-control that threatened to boil over at any moment. It was only by straining his will power to the limit that he succeeded in recovering the pose of mountainous boredom that he usually struggled in vain to maintain in the Saint's maddeningly nonchalant presence.

"I don't know what you hope to gain by all this, Templar, but you're wasting your breath," he said, shifting his lump of worn-out spearmint from one side of his mouth to the other. "I'm acting on facts that even you can't get away from. You may as well know that Sergeant Barrow was in the Dorchester at the time."

"Keeping a fatherly eye on me?"

"No; he was looking for someone else that we're interested in. But that's neither here nor there. Barrow happened to see Miss Avery, and for reasons which I'm not going to explain he kept his eye on her."

"I only hope his thoughts were pure," said the Saint piously.

"Barrow saw you take a package from Miss Avery, and immediately afterwards he saw her leave the restaurant," continued Mr Teal coldly. "He accosted her in the foyer—"

"Disgusting, I call it," said the Saint. "What these policemen get away with—"

"He showed her his authority—"

"She must have been thrilled," murmured Simon.

"She refused to say anything, and Barrow rang me up," went on Teal, his self-control gradually slipping and his voice taking on its familiar blare. "I got hold of these warrants, but I went to Miss Avery's flat first. She denied knowing anything about the Z-Man, but I'd been expecting that. What I did make her admit was that the package she handed you contained a large sum of money."

"Ten thousand pounds," said the Saint lazily. "I counted it."

Teal glowered at him, popeyed.

"I want that package—"

"Sorry, old dear," said the Saint regretfully. "I haven't got it."

"You haven't got it!" brayed Mr Teal.

"Calm yourself, sweetheart," drawled the Saint. "Much as I hate parting with perfectly good boodle when it's pushed right into my hand, I realized that a mistake had been made. Always the perfect gentleman, I immediately took steps to correct the error. On my way home I stopped at a District Messenger office and bunged the package back to Miss Avery, with contents intact. So you see, Claud, old thing, you'll have to tear those warrants up and go back to the assistant commissioner and let him flay you alive. And now that that's all cleared up, what about a smoke and a drink?"

He flicked open his cigarette case with one hand and indicated the whisky decanter with the other. Hoppy Uniatz, aware of the decanter's presence for the first time, moved mechanically towards it, licking his dry lips. Mr Teal, who had been unravelling his tonsils from his epiglottis, lumbered forward like a migrating volcano.

"You're not getting away like that this time, Templar," he said thickly. "You're coming with me! We've been after the Z-Man for a long time, and now we've got him. Are you coming quietly?"

"About as quietly as a brass band," answered the Saint succinctly. "But you needn't blow your whistles and bring in a troop of rozzers. I'm not going to pull a gun on you or start any roughhouse. I know it's a serious thing to interfere with an officer of the law in the execution of his duty—even when he's a mahogany-headed dope with barnacles all over his brain like you are. You say you're armed to the molars with warrants, or else I'd just bounce you out on your fat stomach and call it a day." His blue eyes rested on Mr Teal like twinkling icicles. "So instead of that I'll give you a chance to save your bacon. Before you commit the unmitigated asininity of arresting me and thereby get yourself slung out of a perfectly good job don't you think you'd better take the one obvious step?"

Nothing was obvious to Mr Teal except that he had got Simon Templar where he wanted him at last. But there was a mocking, buccaneering challenge in the Saint's voice that could not go unanswered.

"What obvious step?" he asked scorchingly. "I've got all the evidence I need—"

"I'm sorry; I forgot for the moment that you're only a detective," Simon apologized. "Let me put it into simple words. My answer to you is that Miss Avery gave me the ten thousand quid by mistake, and I rectified the mistake by immediately sending the money back to her. She's bound to have received it by now—and I know she's on the telephone. Since she seems to be the only important witness against me wouldn't it be rather a good idea to make quite certain that all this beautiful evidence of yours is really in the bag?"

He indicated his own instrument and his meaning was clear enough. But Chief Inspector Teal merely grunted and opened the handcuffs.

"That's an old one, isn't it?" he said contemptuously. "While I'm fooling about with the telephone you make your getaway. I'm surprised that you should suggest such a whiskery—"

He was interrupted by the shrill ringing of the twin bells of the telephone, and the Saint automatically reached for the instrument.

"No, you don't!" barked Mr Teal. "I'll take it."

Simon couldn't help smiling, for the detective was doing the very thing he had just been sneering at. But the Saint had no desire to make a getaway. He had a hunch that he knew where that call was coming from.

"Hullo!" said Mr Teal in a carefully controlled, Saintly voice.

"Is that Mr Simon Templar?"

"Yes," replied Mr Teal untruthfully; and he experienced a sudden awful feeling as though somebody had removed his stomach in one piece, leaving a wide open space; for the voice at the other end of the wire belonged unmistakably to Beatrice Avery. Mr Teal went to the movies often enough to know that.

"I owe you a humble apology, Mr Templar, for making such a stupid mistake," said Beatrice Avery, and Mr Teal heard the words through a kind of infernal tantara, in which the assistant commissioner's eloquent sniff was the most easily recognizable sound. "Thank you a thousand times for sending the money back so promptly. It was all a silly joke. Please forgive me."

III

If there was any joke in sight it was beyond the range of Mr Teal's sense of humour. He stood clinging to the telephone like a drowning man attached to a waterlogged straw. However it had been managed, somehow it had been done again: the Saint had been right in his hands and had slipped through them like a trickle of water. It was impossible, incredible, inhuman, unfair, unjust—but it had happened. Teal's head buzzed with the petrifying impact of the blow. He swallowed voicelessly, trying to think of something to say or do, but his brain seemed to be taking a temporary siesta. All he could think of was that he wanted to find some peaceful place in which to die. And at the same time he was bitterly aware that the Saint would probably still be capable of making him turn in his grave.

The Saint had enough confirmation of his hunch in the expression on Mr Teal's stricken face. He took the receiver gently out of the detective's hand and placed it to his own ear.

"I was half expecting you to ring, fair lady," he said easily. "If ever we meet again I hope you will make full compensation for that look you gave me—"

"I just told you, Mr Templar, that it was only a silly joke," interrupted the girl's breathless voice. "Please forget all about it."

"That's not so easy. If there's anything I could do to help—"

"Help?" The girl forced a laugh, and to the Saint it

sounded almost hysterical. "Why should I want any help? It was just an idiotic practical joke, and it went wrong. That's all, Mr Templar. I'm afraid I made a dreadful little fool of myself, and I shall be eternally grateful if you'll forget the whole thing."

"Is it as bad as that, darling?" Simon asked softly. "Because—"

"Thank you so much, Mr Templar. Good-bye."

Simon slid a cigarette into his mouth as he turned away from the instrument. In the fuliginous silence that followed, as the Saint lighted his smoke, Chief Inspector Teal's pudgy fingers slowly and laboriously unwrapped a fresh wafer of spearmint. Mr Teal was making a game effort to recover his composure, and it was brutally hard going. He was tied in a knot, and he knew it. It was an old, old knot, and he was familiar with every twist of it. Once again he had believed that triumph was within his grasp, and once again that debonair outlaw had cheated him. And it would happen again and again and again and forever. The knowledge percolated into Mr Teal's interior like a liquid cannon ball, solidifying into its original shape in the lower region of his stomach. He thrust the wafer of gum into his mouth and glared murderously at the unemotional Sergeant Barrow.

"Well?" he demanded sulphurously. "What are we waiting for?"

"Don't take it so much to heart, Claud, old dear," said the Saint, his voice surprisingly innocent of raillery. "Don't be in a hurry to dash off either. You're not bursting with anxiety to have that chat with the assistant commissioner, are you? I'm not going to prod you in the waistcoat—"

"You'd better not try!" said Mr Teal hoarsely as he shifted his ample paunch well out of range of the Saint's questing forefinger.

"Have a drink, and let's get together," pleaded the Saint. "The mistake you made was natural enough—and if the worst comes to the worst you can always shove the blame onto Sergeant Barrow. You probably will anyhow. But that doesn't make it up to me. The thing which pains me is that you should have mistaken me for this bird of prey who calls himself the Z-Man. A bloke who can cause a girl full of charm and glamour and a hard-boiled detective to frizzle me with a couple of looks like the interior of a sewage incinerator must be pretty epizootic. Tell me, Claud, who is this descendant of Dracula?"

But something else had settled upon Mr Teal's tortured presence—something oddly stubborn and impenetrable that didn't fit in with his earlier demonstrations any more than it belonged to the stunned paralysis which had since overcome him. It was as if he had drawn back inside himself and locked a door.

"Forget it," he said stonily.

"I can't forget something I don't know. Be reasonable, dear old nitwit. It's only fair to me—"

"I don't know anything about the Z-Man, and nobody else knows anything about the Z-Man," Teal said deliberately. "I was just trying to be funny. Understand?"

He nodded sleepily, jerked his head towards Sergeant Barrow, and they both left. As the front door gave a vicious slam Hoppy Uniatz reached for the whisky decanter and thrust the neck of it into his capacious mouth.

"Boss," he said, coming to the surface, "I don't get nut'n."

"Except the whisky," murmured the Saint, rescuing the decanter. "For once, Hoppy, I'm right in your street. I don't get nut'n either."

"Why ja let dem bums get away wit' it?" asked Mr Uniatz discontentedly. "Dey got a noive, bustin' in like dat. Say, if we knew some politicians we could have dose mugs walkin' a beat again so fast—"

Simon was not listening. He was pacing up and down like a tiger, inhaling deeply from his cigarette; and as Mr Uniatz watched him a slow smile of appreciation illuminated his homely face. He could see that his boss was thinking, and, knowing from his own experience what a painful ordeal this was, he relapsed into a sympathetic and respectful silence.

It was clear enough to the Saint that Mr Teal had been disturbed by certain dimensions of his blunder which hadn't been apparent at first sight. The very existence of the Z-Man, it seemed, had been a closely guarded secret—until Teal had let the cat peep out of the bag and wink at Simon Templar, of all people. Unable to undo the damage which he had done in his first excess of confidence, the detective had taken the only remedy he had left and had escaped from the Saint's magnetic presence before he could be lured into any more mistakes. But as far as the Saint was concerned he had still left plenty of interesting ideas behind him.

A key turned in the front door, and a moment later Patricia Holm walked into the living room. She looked at the Saint accusingly.

"I met Teal downstairs," she said. "What are we going to be arrested for now?"

"Nothing," answered the Saint peacefully. "Claud Eustace thought I was, though, until I showed him the error of his ways. Sit down, lass, and listen to the tale of how a perfectly respectable buccaneer was mistaken for the ungodliest of the ungodly."

Patricia sat down with the patience that she had learned through years of testing it. She had known the Saint too long to be surprised by any story he had to tell; and she knew him too well to be deceived by the

transparency of his present calm. There was the unmistakable hell-for-leather lilt in his voice, hinting at battle,
murder and sudden death; and when that lilt was there
it was as useless to oppose him as it would have been
useless to argue with a cyclone.

"We're going after the Z-Man," he said dreamily.

"Who's the Z-Man?"

"I don't know."

"That ought to give us a flying start then," said Patricia kindly. "Do you know what it's all about, Hoppy?"

"I don't know nut'n," answered Mr Uniatz as though
he were a phonograph record with a crack in it.

It didn't take the Saint long to give a full and vivid
recital of what he knew. He was always fond of his own
voice, but this time there wasn't much for him to tell.
The girl listened with growing interest; but at the finish,
when he asked for her opinion, she had none to offer.

"You still don't really know anything," she objected.

"Exactly," agreed the Saint, unabashed. "It was only
by chance that I heard anything about the Z-Man at all—
and that was mostly because Claud dropped a brick. It's
just another proof, Pat, old cherub, that my guardian
angel never falls down on the job. Something tells me
that this game is Big, and I should be lacking in moral
duty if I didn't sit in on it. Observe the reactions of
Beatrice Avery and Claud Eustace Teal—two people who
have just about as much in common as a gazelle and a
hippopotamus. Both of them closed up as enthusiasti-
cally as a couple of lively clams. Both of them refused to
discuss the subject of the Z-Man. Both of them told me
it was all a joke."

The Saint rose to his feet and lighted another cigarette. His eyes were mere slits of steel.

"A joke!" he repeated. "If you'd seen the look in
Beatrice Avery's eyes, Pat, you'd know how much of a

joke the Z-Man is! Teal, too. He was fool enough to think I was the Z-Man, and he didn't want to put the bracelets on me because he'd have to touch me! By God, this bird must be something that'd make Jack the Ripper look like a Salvation Army drummer boy."

"You still don't know anything useful," Patricia said practically. "What are you going to do—advertise for him?"

"I don't know. . . . There's a hell of a lot I don't know," answered the Saint, scowling. "I don't even know what the Z-Man's racket is—excepting that it must be damned profitable. It's no good asking Teal for information; he's in trouble enough already. I can't go to Beatrice Avery—or at least, if I did she wouldn't see me or tell me anything."

"She might see me."

"She won't see anybody," said the Saint. "After what has happened today she'll be scared as stiff as a corpse. Don't you get it, darling? She had an appointment with the Z-Man or one of his agents, and she knows she failed to keep it. The Z-Man won't know that she actually *did* keep it, and he'll start turning on the heat. This girl will have extra locks and bolts on her doors—"

"Didn't you say that she and I look a bit alike?"

"Only in height and build and fair-headedness and general beauty and all that sort of thing," replied Simon. "You're both the same type, that's all."

"Then leave it to me," said Patricia calmly. "I'll show you what a real detective can do."

It was the conventional tea hour when she entered the handsome new apartment house in the neighbourhood of Marble Arch known as Parkside Court. Number 21 was on the sixth floor, and Patricia went up in the elevator in spite of the fact that the porter had warned her that Miss Avery had given instructions that she was not at home to anybody. The porter had put it more broadly than this; he had declared that Miss Avery had gone down to Cornwall for a holiday—or up into Aberdeenshire, he wasn't sure which. But Patricia had looked at him with her sapphire-blue eyes, so remarkably like the Saint's, and her bewitching smile, and the unfortunate man had dried completely up.

In the carpeted corridor, outside the door of number 21 a man was repairing a vacuum cleaner. Patricia was sorry for him. He had taken the vacuum cleaner apart into so many pieces that it was very doubtful whether it could ever be put together again. Notwithstanding his workmanlike overalls, Patricia had no difficulty in recognizing him as an employee of some private detective agency. He had "ex-policeman" stamped all over him in embossed lettering.

"No good you ringing that bell, miss," he said gruffly as Patricia placed her finger on the button. "There's nobody at home. Miss Avery's gone into the country."

He had looked at her very hard at first with a somewhat startled expression on his face. Patricia knew why. She went on smiling at him.

"Is there any special way of ringing?" she enquired sweetly. "I don't think she'll refuse to see her own sister."

The man suddenly grinned.

"Well, of course that's different, miss," he said hastily. "I thought there was a likeness. Why, when you came round the corner I took you for Miss Avery herself."

He gave three short rings, a long one and three more short. The door was almost immediately opened by a nervous-looking maid.

"Okay, Bessie, it's Miss Avery's sister."

Patricia walked straight in, just as the Saint might have done, and her complete assurance gave the maid no chance to reply. A moment later, in the artistically lighted living room, she was face to face with Beatrice Avery.

"I'm quite harmless, and I hope you'll forgive me for getting in by a trick, Miss Avery," she said directly. She opened her bag and produced a card. "This will tell you who I am—and perhaps you'll guess why I'm here."

The film star's frightened eyes looked up from the card.

"Yes, I've heard your name," she whispered. "You work with the Saint, don't you? Sit down, please, Miss Holm. I don't know why you've come. I told Mr Templar over the phone that it was all a silly joke—"

"And I'm here because the Saint didn't believe you," Patricia interrupted gently. "If you've heard of him you must know that you can trust him. Simon thinks that something ought to be done about the Z-Man, and he's the one man in all the world to do it."

Beatrice Avery's breasts stirred shakily under her clinging satin negligee, and her grey eyes grew obstinate—with the dreadful obstinacy of utter fear.

"It's all very absurd, Miss Holm," she said, trying to speak carelessly. "There's no such person as the Z-Man. How did Mr Templar know . . . I mean, there's nothing I can tell you."

"You'd rather pay ten thousand pounds—"

"There's nothing I can tell you," repeated the girl, rising to her feet. "Nothing! Nothing at all! Please leave me alone!"

Her voice was almost shrill, and Patricia saw at a glance that it would be hopeless to prolong the interview. Beatrice Avery was a great deal more frightened than even the Saint had realized or Patricia had expected. Patricia was shrewd and understanding, and she knew when she was wasting her time. Anybody less clever would have persisted and only hardened Beatrice Avery's obstinacy. All Patricia did was to point to her card on the table.

"If you change your mind," she said, "there's the phone number. We'll do anything we can to help you—and we keep secrets."

She was not feeling very satisfied with herself as she rode down in the elevator. It wouldn't be pleasant to go back to the Saint and report failure after the boast she had made. But it couldn't be helped. It was just one of those things. The Saint would think of some other approach. . . .

The hall was deserted when she reached it, and she walked out into the evening dusk and paused uncertainly on the sidewalk in the glow of the red and green neon lights that decorated the entrance. A taxi crawled by, and she signalled. The driver swung round in the road and pulled in.

"Cornwall House, Piccadilly," said Patricia.

"Yes, miss," answered the driver, reaching round and opening the door.

She got in, and the cab was off before she had fairly closed the door. Something hard and round pressed into her side, and she looked quickly into the shadows. A smallish man with ferretlike eyes was sitting beside her.

"One scream, sister, and you're for it," said the man in a flat matter-of-fact voice. "This thing in your side is a gun, and I'm not afraid to use it."

"Oh!" said Patricia faintly, and she sagged into limpness.

She had done it so well that Ferret Eyes was completely taken in. Patricia, her brain working like oiled machinery, did not blame herself for having fallen into such a simple trap. She had had no reason to be on the alert for one; and she knew that it had not been laid for her at all. The ungodly had mistaken her for Beatrice

Avery! And why shouldn't they? She was the same height and colouring, close enough to have deceived even the Saint at a distance, and she had emerged from the apartment house where Beatrice Avery lived. With the added help of the dim light she might have deceived anyone—and might go on deceiving him for a while, so long as she kept her mouth shut. It was to avoid being forced to talk too much that she had feigned that rapid faint, to give herself a chance to think over her next move.

She was aware of a throb of excitement within her. There was no fear in her—the Saint had taught her to forget such things. Instead he had bequeathed her so much of his own blithe recklessness that she saw in a flash that while she had failed with Beatrice Avery she might yet succeed in this new and unexpected quarter. It amused her to think that while the enemy wouldn't have dared to use the taxicab trick with her, they had thought it good enough for the film star, who was naturally unversed in the ways of the ungodly. And yet it was she, Patricia Holm, who had fallen for it! It was a twist that might provide the Saint with the scent he was looking for.

She was preparing to come naturally out of her faint when the taxi bumped heavily and swung giddily round in a sharp arc. Then it came to a jerky stop, and Pat heard some doors closing. She sat half forward with a dazed look on her face.

"Take it easy, sister," said Ferret Eyes gratingly. "Nobody's going to hurt that lovely face of yours—yet."

"Where am I? What are you going to do to me?" she gasped, her voice faltering. "I'll pay!" she went on hysterically. "I tried to pay at the Dorchester. You didn't come. I had the money—"

"Tell it to somebody else," he said callously.

He forced her to get out, and she saw that the cab

He was disappointed, however, in assuming that this would result in a decrease in the cellar's illumination. The general lighting effect was not only doubled, but he himself stood in the direct glare of a miniature searchlight. The Saint had decided that it was time to take full stock of the situation, and his own flashlight was even better than the one that had gone out.

The man who had stood concealed behind the light was a disappointment. His appearance, after the crisp and authoritative tone of his voice, came as a considerable shock. He was a small skinny bird of about forty, extraordinarily neatly dressed, his ornamentations including a waisted overcoat and fawn spats. His face was small featured with sandy eyebrows just visible over the tops of his highly respectable gold-rimmed pince-nez. His nose and mouth were small; and his chin, after a half-hearted attempt to establish itself, drifted away to hide itself shyly in his neck.

"You ought to be more careful, Andy," Simon admonished him. "Take that gun out of your pocket if you like, but spread it out on the floor where we can all feast our eyes on it."

"My name is not Andy," said the chinless man.

"No? Except for the eye gear and the spats you look exactly like Andy Gump," answered the Saint. "Pat, old darling, if you can spare a moment you might build up our collection of artillery."

Not one of the men attempted to move. They knew the Saint's reputation, and they had an earnest and unanimous desire to continue living. Behind the bantering cadence of the Saint's voice there was a glacial chill that converted the cellar into a refrigerator. His gun was extremely visible, too, and the lean brown fingers that held it had a lively quality that made them look as if they would just as soon start squeezing as keep still.

Patricia relieved the clerkly-looking Mr Gump of his gun, and Ferret Eyes threw his own weapon on the floor before she could even turn to him.

"I ain't got no pistol, miss, swelp me I ain't," swore the taxi driver hoarsely.

She believed him, but she patted his pockets just the same. And Simon descended the stairs.

"Now, boys, you can line yourselves up against that wall over there," he said with an indicative flick of his gun muzzle. "And don't forget where you are. . . . Pat, you take this heater and stand well to the side. Here's the torch, too, and keep the light nicely steady. . . . It will interest you birds to know," he added for the benefit of the obedient trio, "that the lady can hit a microbe's eye at fifty yards. If you don't believe me, you only have to bring on your microbes."

He took Mr Gump's gun from Patricia and picked up Ferret Eyes' weapon from the floor; then he swiftly examined both and thrust them into his pocket. From another pocket he produced a second automatic of his own. He never trusted strange weapons. Holding his gun with careless ease, he briefly inspected the taxi driver and Ferret Eyes; he was not particularly interested in either of them since they definitely came within the dull category of small fry. Mr G————

...ose to the Z-Man. Mr Gump needed careful investigation. He looked very meek and inoffensive as the Saint started going through his pockets—except perhaps for the snakelike glitter in his eyes behind the gold-rimmed pince-nez—a glitter which belied the disarming weakness of his chin.

And suddenly Mr Gump gave a demonstration which proved him to be either a very rash fool or a very brave man. As Simon Templar was in the act of insinuating a brown hand into Mr Gump's breast pocket a knee shot up and dug itself into the lower region of his stomach. With a simultaneous cohesion of movement Mr Gump grabbed at the Saint's gun and tore it out of Simon's relaxed fingers. In another instant the muzzle was jammed hard against Simon's chest with Mr Gump's finger on the trigger.

"Drop that gun, Miss Holm, or your friend becomes an angel instead of a Saint," said Mr Gump.

Patricia made no movement. Nobody made any movement. And the Saint chuckled.

"That was careless of me, brother—but not so careless as you think," he murmured. "That gun's the one I didn't load."

He raised his hand almost casually and took hold of Mr Gump's small nose. He gripped it very hard between his finger and thumb and twisted it.

Click!

Mr Gump pulled the trigger in a flurry of blind fury and extreme anguish. And that empty *click!* was the only result. He pulled again, and nothing happened. Nothing, that is, except that the agonizing torque on his sensitive nose increased. He let out a strangled squeal and dropped his useless weapon; and at the same time the Saint released his grip.

"I told you it wasn't loaded," said the Saint, picking up the automatic by the trigger guard and dropping it into his pocket. "I think I'd better use your gun, Andy. But don't try any more tricks like that, or I might really have to hurt you."

Mr Gump did not reply; except for the baleful glitter in his streaming eyes he seemed unmoved. Patricia who knew the Saint's twisted sense of humour better than anybody, wondered why he had wasted time by amusing himself so childishly at Mr Gump's expense. There must have been a reason somewhere; for Simon Templar never did strange things without a reason, and it was invariably a good one. It was noticeable that he held the new gun, which was loaded with death, in such a way that Mr Gump would never have a chance of grabbing it.

"So we collect pretty pictures, do we?"

The Saint's voice held nothing but tolerant amusement as he inspected the four glossy photographs of feminine pulchritude which he had abstracted from Mr Gump's breast pocket.

"Why not?" said the other defensively. "I'm a film fan."

"Brother, you certainly know how to pick winners," commented the Saint. "This young lady in the voluminous mid-Victorian attire, complete with bustle, is undoubtedly Miss Beatrice Avery, shining star of Triumph Film Productions Limited. Very charming. Of course it's her you thought you were snatching tonight. Number Two, in the exotic Eastern outfit, is the lovely Irene Cromwell, under contract with Pyramid Pictures. We could use her, Andy. Number Three, in the dinky abbreviated beach suit, is no less a person than Sheila Ireland, now starring with Summit Picture Corporation. I can see I shall have to get out my old water wings. And Number Four—" He paused, and his eyes hardened. "Very sad about Number Four, don't you think, Andy? A couple of months ago Miss Mercia Landon was doing the final scenes of her new film for Atlantic Studios. A couple of months ago . . . And now?"

"I don't know what you're getting at," said Mr Gump woodenly.

"If you don't the Z-Man is very careless in choosing his assistants," answered the Saint.

"What the hell do you mean?" stammered the chinless man, his inward alarm crashing suddenly through the veneer of calm which he had tried to preserve. "There's no harm in my carrying those photographs. Anybody can get them. I'm a film fan—"

"So you told me," agreed the Saint, slipping the photographs into his own pocket. "And a kidnapper in your spare time, too, by the looks of it," he added casually. "Well, I may as well see what the rest of your hobbies are—although I'm not likely to find anything half so interesting as your favourite film stars."

He put a cigarette into his mouth, lighted it with a match which he sprung into flame with his thumbnail and set it at a rakish angle. If the men before him had known him better they would have sweated with fear, for that rakish slant was an infallible sign that something was going to happen and that he was personally going to start it. Patricia felt her heart beating a shade faster. Except for the one danger signal there was nothing to give her a clue to what was in his mind.

He completed the search, finding cigarettes, matches, money, keys and all the usual contents of an average man's pockets, but nothing to reveal Mr Gump's real identity and nothing to connect him with the mysterious Z-Man. Even the tailor's label inside his breast pocket had been removed.

"Well, gents, we can call it an evening." The Saint wavered his gun muzzle gently over the three men. "Pat, old thing, sling me the torch and then get up to the garage. We've finished here."

She obeyed at once; and a moment later Simon himself was backing up the stairs, keeping his flashlight flooding downwards. As soon as he reached the top he swung the door to and fastened it. It was not a good door. There were cracks in it, the hinges were old and rusted, and the lock had long since ceased to function; but the Saint overcame these trifling drawbacks by the simple expedient of propping three or four heavy wooden stacks against the door. Since it opened outwards the three musketeers would have to work for some time before they could make their escape.

"We have been having a lot of luck lately, haven't we?" Patricia remarked philosophically.

"Have I grumbled?" asked the Saint, making no attempt to lower his voice—and, indeed, speaking quite close to the barricaded cellar door. "We're going to shoot off to Parkside Court now, old dear, and warn Beatrice Avery that she'd better be packing. After what happened to you it's pretty obvious that the ungodly are likely to put in some fast work, and we're going to be just one move ahead of them. If necessary we'll take the fair Beatrice away by force."

"Why didn't you question those fellows about the Z-Man?"

"They wouldn't have come through with a syllable unless I'd beaten it out of them, and I'm not in one of my torturing moods this evening," answered Simon. "Don't worry about the Three Little Pigs—it'll take them about an hour to get out, and I doubt if they'll go after Beatrice again tonight anyway. Ready, darling?"

While he spoke he had been flashing his torch about the garage. There was a telephone in one corner, and this interested him for a moment; but a few odd potatoes lying on the floor against one of the walls interested him almost as much. He picked up the biggest he could find and bent down at the rear of the taxi to jam the providential tuber firmly over the end of the exhaust pipe.

"All set, keed," he murmured, and his eyes were bright with mischief.

V

The men in the cellar heard the main garage door creak open and then close. After that there was a large silence, broken at last by Ferret Eyes. Exactly what he said is immaterial. Ninety percent of it would have burned holes through any printed page, and the subject matter in between the frankly irrelevant patches cast grievous aspersions on Simon Templar's parentage, his physical characteristics and his purely personal habits. The air of the cellar was rapidly turning a deep blue when the chinless man cut in.

"It's no good cursing the Saint," he said sharply. "The mistake was yours, Welmont, and you know it. Why don't you try cursing yourself?"

"What's Z going to say?" asked Welmont, a frightened note coming into his voice. "It wasn't my fault, Raddon. Damn it, you can't blame me. From the other side of road the girl looked exactly like Beatrice Avery. How the hell was I to know? She came out of Parkside Court—"

"Save it until later." Raddon cut him off impatiently. "The first thing we've got to do is to get out of here. See what you can do with the door, Tyler. You know more about this damn place than I do."

The taxi driver mounted the stairs and heaved against the door. It creaked and groaned but gave no sign of opening.

"It's jammed," he reported unnecessarily. "The lock's no good, and there ain't any bolts. That ruddy perisher must have done somethink." He swore comprehensively. "Now we're in a ruddy mess, ain't we? I told yer not to bring that ruddy jane to my garridge."

It was not the best of all places for applying force. The stairs were narrow and steep and slippery, and there was no possible way of exerting leverage or even making a shoulder charge. It was equally impossible for two men to stand side by side. Raddon himself went up and examined the door, holding the torch to the cracks so that the beam of light passed through.

"There's only one way to get out," he said. "If we cut away the lower part of the door we can use a plank to shift the props. There are two or three planks lying in the cellar against the wall. You'd better start, Tyler."

The taxi driver cursed and grumbled but set to work. The door was old and misshapen, but it was tough. Tyler and Welmont, working in turn while Raddon held the light, took the better part of half an hour to break through. They had only penknives for tools, and they had to split and chip away the wood in fragments. Finally Tyler forced one of his heavy boots through the opening with a vicious kick. A plank was then thrust through and the props dislodged.

" 'S'pose 'e sends the rozzers?" asked the driver anxiously. "I'll lose my license, that's wot I'll don. I was a ruddy fool to let you use my garridge."

"If Templar had sent the police they'd have been here twenty minutes ago," Raddon answered promptly. "The Saint doesn't want the police in this any more than we do. But he's an interfering swine, and we've got to get after him. Start up the cab, Tyler."

"Give me a charnce, will yer?" protested Tyler, climbing into his seat. "I'll 'ave it out in a jiffy."

He was an optimist. They gave him a chance; but the self-starter, which usually had the engine firing after the first whirr, whirred in vain. Tyler's cursing only added to the ear-aching sounds which filled the garage.

"You'll have no batteries left," Raddon said helpfully.

The taxi man climbed down from his seat.

"Funny bloomin' thing," he rumbled. "She don't usually play tricks like this 'ere. 'Tain't as if she was stone cold neither."

"Perhaps you forgot to turn the petrol on," ventured Welmont.

"P'raps there ain't any blinkin' engine," snarled Tyler. "Wot the 'ell d' yer take me for?" He uncovered the engine and addressed a few scorching remarks to it. "Can't nobody show me a light?" he said bitterly. "Think I'm a blarsted cat? Nothink wrong with the jooce." The carburetor flooded at his touch. "Ignition looks all right too. 'E didn't take out the plugs. Nothink loose nowhere. . . ."

He tried again, with the same result. The engine, for some inexplicable reason, amused itself by turning over, but it simply refused to fire. Tyler had been a taxi driver for years, and before that he had worked as a motor mechanic. The cab was his own property, and he always did his own repairs. He tried everything he could think of, but he never thought of taking a look at the rear end of the exhaust pipe.

"We've wasted enough time," said Raddon angrily. "I've got to get in touch with Z—"

He broke off as he caught sight of the telephone in the corner. It was only by chance that he had seen it at all, for it was almost hidden behind a number of ancient and ragged tires which hung on the wall, and Welmont's torchlight had swung in that direction quite casually and without any intentional objective. Raddon's eyes narrowed behind the gold-rimmed pince-nez, and he flashed his own torch into the corner.

"Is this phone connected?" he asked sharply.

"Wot the 'ell d' yer mean?" Tyler demanded, looking round indignantly. "Think I ain't paid the rent for it? Of course it's connected."

"Why didn't you tell me it was here?" Raddon retorted. "I could have used it long ago. Now it may be too late. . . . You heard what Templar said to the Holm girl before they left?"

He went to the instrument, held his light steadily on it and dialled Scotland Yard. As soon as the switchboard operator answered he spoke in a deep voice with a forced foreign inflection.

"Take this down garefully," he said distinctly. "Simon Templar, alias the Saint, alias the Z-Man, is at this moment gidnabbing Beatrice Avery, the film star, from her apartment in Barkside Gourt. That's all."

He hung up before the operator could answer.

"'Ere, wot abaht me?" demanded Tyler frantically. "You got a ruddy nerve, usin' my phone for that job. They can trace that call. Think I want the cops round 'ere arskin' questions?"

"You know nothing about it," said Raddon calmly. "You left the garage unlocked, and somebody used your phone. What does it matter, you fool? They can't pin anything on you. I had to get through to the Yard at once. If they pull Templar in he'll spend the next two weeks trying to explain his movements. The Yard's been trying to get him for years, and if they catch him red-handed snatching the Avery girl they'll send him up for a ten-year stretch."

He turned to the instrument again and flashed his light on the dial. Placing his body between the telephone and the other two men so that they could not watch the movements of his finger, he quickly dialled another number and waited. He listened to the steady "burr-burr" for a few moments, and then a voice answered.

"Raddon here," he said in a rapid subdued voice. "Something has gone wrong. Can't do anything more this evening. Better turn our attention to the next proposition. . . ." He broke off and listened. "All right. Usual place tomorrow, as early as possible."

He hung up at once and found Welmont looking curiously at him out of his ferret eyes.

"Was that Z?" Welmont asked.

"It was Gandhi," answered Raddon curtly. "If you're ready we'll go. There's nothing more for tonight. Too dangerous to move until we know more about Templar."

They departed—none too soon for Tyler, who was jumpy and worried—leaving one of the big double doors slightly ajar.

Simon Templar stroked the cog of his lighter and inhaled deeply and luxuriously from a much-needed cigarette. He heard the three men walking over the cobbles outside; and then silence. With the lithe ease of a panther he lowered himself from the overhead beam on which he had been lying at full length, dropped to the roof of the taxi and thence descended to the ground.

There was a smile on his lips as he dusted himself down. That beam, so easily reached from the roof of the taxi, had positively asked him to make its aquaintance when he had first glanced up at it. Patricia, he knew, could handle her end of the job with smooth efficiency; he had had a couple of minutes earnest talk with her before they parted. For Simon Templar, even before he left the cellar, had put in some of that characteristic quick thinking which was the everlasting despair of the law and the ungodly alike. His restless brain, working at supercharged pressure, had looked into the immediate future with a clarity that was little short of clairvoyant; he had formulated a plan of action out of a situation that had not even acquired a definite geography. But that power of thinking ahead into the most remote possibilities was the gift which had so often left his enemies breathless in the background, hopelessly outpaced by the hurricane speed of the Saint's imagination. . . .

Which satisfactorily explains why he was still in

Mr Tyler's garage, dusting the well-creased knees of his impeccable Anderson & Sheppard trousers and by no means dissatisfied with the results of his roosting. He grinned helplessly as he realized how easily the departed trio could have seen him if they had only looked up into the dusty rafters. Not that it would have mattered much: he was armed, and they weren't. However, it was just as well that he had remained undiscovered. His ears hadn't told him much more than he knew already; but his eyes had served him well.

Raddon's phone call to Scotland Yard had given him nothing to worry about. If he knew anything of Patricia she would be through with Beatrice Avery long before the padded shoulders of the law could darken the portals of Parkside Court.

His eyes had served him on the second phone call. Lying along the overhead beam, he had looked straight down on the telephone. . . . He chuckled as he thought of Raddon's precautions. Raddon would never have used the instrument at all for his second call if it had been one of the old-fashioned non-dialing type. He couldn't have given his number to the exchange without giving it to Welmont and Tyler at the same time. Dialling was different: he had only to obtrude his body between his companions and the telephone, and they couldn't possibly know what number he had called.

But the Saint, with a perfect bird's-eye view, had watched every movement of Raddon's fingers on the dial: his supersensitive ears had listened to every click of the returning disc; he had memorized the number and tucked it securely away in a corner of his retentive brain. Raddon's finger had first jabbed into the PRS hole, then into the ABC, then into the PRS again. This could only mean one exchange—PAR, otherwise PARliament. The numbers were easy, Raddon had called PARliament 5577.

The Z-Man's telephone number! Or, at least, a number he was in the practice of using.

There were ways and means of discovering to whom that number had been allocated. Searching through the London Telephone Directory was one of them, but the Saint had never been able to rave about that particularly tedious occupation. There were easier methods. One of them he tried at once. He dialled PARliament 5577 himself and blew smoke rings at the mouthpiece while he waited. His connection came quickly, and a thick voice said:

"Vell?"

"The same to you, comrade," said the Saint fraternally. "Kindly put me through to Mr Thistlethwaite—"

"Vot? Der iss nobody named that," said the thick voice.

"You'll pardon me, but there's a very large somebody named that," said the Saint firmly. "Senior partner of the firm of Thistlethwaite and Abernethy—"

"This iss not the firm you say."

"No? Then who is it?" asked the Saint obstinately. "What's the idea of using Thistlethwaite and Abernethy's telephone number? Aren't you Parliament 5577?"

"Yes."

"Then don't be silly. You're Thistlethwaite. Or are you Abernethy?"

"Ve are not dose names," shouted the thick voice.

The line became dead, but Simon Templar was not discouraged. He had not expected to click at the first attempt. He dialled the number a second time and waited.

"Vell?"

"Oh, it's you again, is it?" said the Saint cheerfully. "Vell—I mean, well, that proves that you *must* be Thistlethwaite. Or else you're Abernethy. I damn well know I dialled the right number."

"Ve are *not* Thistle-vot-you-say und somebody," roared the thick voice, its owner clearly under the impression that he was dealing with a genial half-wit. "You got the wrong number again, you fool!"

"If you're Parliament 5577 you're Thistlethwaite and Abernethy," insisted the Saint. "Think I don't know?"

"Ve are Zeidelmann und Co.," bellowed the angry voice, "und ve know nothing of the peoples you say."

"Well I'm damned!" said Simon in surprise. "Then am I the bloke who's been making the mistake? A thousand apologies, dear old frankfurter. And the same to Co."

He hung up, and with his cigarette slanting dangerously out of the corner of his mouth he turned over the last few pages of Vol. II of the London Telephone Directory, which lay on a shelf. There was only one Zeidelmann & Co.; and the address was Bryerby House, Victoria.

The Saint paused for a moment to remove the potato from the taxicab's exhaust pipe, and as he strode silently down a long narrow yard with high walls on either side he reflected on the absurdity of a mere humble potato rendering impotent one of man's greatest mechanical wonders. And at the same time he reflected on his own remarkable good fortune. Beyond any shadow of doubt, his guardian angel was having a busy day. . . .

VI

He was somewhere in the Cricklewood district, and he found his great cream-and-red Hirondel parked where he had left it. His opportune arrival in the garage cellar a little earlier had been no coincidence. He had allowed Patricia Holm to go to Parkside Court alone, but he had hovered cautiously in the offing himself, and it had been a simple matter to follow the taxi which had started off with such suspicious abruptness.

"The Z-Man—Zeidelmann & Co.," he said to himself as he drove swiftly towards Victoria. "Significant—and yet rather too easy. There's a catch in it somewhere."

Bryerby House stood in a quiet road off Victoria Street. Simon parked his car near by and walked to the office building. He had formulated no plan of action, but doubtless something would occur to him when it was necessary. Direct action, the straightforward and devastatingly simple approach which had always appealed to him, continued to offer tempting possibilities. It looked as if Zeidelmann & Co. had something to do with the Z-Man. Therefore he wanted to feast his eyes on Zeidelmann & Co. The logic of the proposition seemed incontrovertible; and as for its consequences, Simon was cheerfully prepared to let the Lord provide.

There was a wicked glimmer of anticipation in his eyes as he inspected the grubby board in the hall on which was painted a list of the occupants and their various callings. Zeidelmann & Co. apparently did nothing for a living, for beyond stating that their office was situated on the ground floor the board was completely dumb. The Saint wandered down a shabby bare-boarded passage, scanning the names on the doors as he passed them. He met nobody, for Bryerby House was one of those janitor-less office buildings in which one could wander unhindered and unchallenged at any hour of the day; and although the evening was quite young it was still old enough for most businessmen to have paddled off to the discomfort of their suburban homes. The passage took a turn at the end, and Simon Templar found himself facing a glass-topped door. There was a light within, and painted on the glass were the illuminating words:

ZEIDELMANN & CO.
Curios

Simon cocked his hat at the sign.

"And indeed they are," he drawled and knocked on the door.

"Vell?" came a familiar thick voice.

"So our old pal Mr Vell is here," murmured the Saint, turning the door handle and entering. "Good evening, Z-Man," he added affably as he closed the door and lounged elegantly against it. "This is the Saint calling. And how's the trade in old pots and pans?"

One hand rested carelessly in his pocket, and the other flicked a cigarette into his mouth and then snapped a match head into flame. His languidly mocking eyes had missed nothing in the first quick survey of the room. The office was small and barren. It contained nothing but a shabby flat-topped desk, a couple of chairs, a table lamp and a telephone. At the desk sat a big shadowy man—the Saint could only see him indistinctly, for the lampshade was tilted over so that the light shone towards the door and left the man at the desk in semigloom. It seemed to be a popular lighting system among the clan.

"*Himmel!* You are the crazy fool who telephoned, yes?"

"Well, I did telephone," Simon admitted. "But I don't know if I'd answer to the rest of it." His gaze swept coolly over the room again. "You must do a thriving business here," he drawled. "I see your stock's pretty well sold out. Or do you mostly keep it in old cellars?"

"Vot you vant mit me?" demanded the other. "Vot iss tiss 'Saint' nonsense? I am Mr Otto Zeidelmann, und you I do not know."

"That's a condition which will be remedied from now onwards, brother," said the Saint pleasantly. "You'll get to know me better every minute. I dropped in this evening to have a look at you, and I must say you're not very obliging. That lampshade—excuse me."

Thud!

Something like a streak of silver lightning hissed across the desk and buried its point in the arm of the chair a fraction of an inch from Mr Zeidelmann's hand, which had been edging towards the centre drawer of the desk.

"I'm getting out of practice," said the Saint regretfully. "I meant that knife to pin your sleeve to the chair."

Mr Zeidelmann looked down at the still quivering ivory hilt and sat as still as a mummified corpse.

"God!" he muttered shakily. "Are you a lunatic?"

"No," said the Saint mildly. "But I'm afraid you'll look like one if you waste any time denying that you're the Z-Man. By the way, did you notice that in your perturbation you said 'God' just now instead of 'Gott'? You want to watch little details like that when you disguise yourself. Respectable manufacturers' agents don't keep guns in their desk drawers, either—or any other kind of drawers, if it comes to that. Besides, I heard Mr Gump—Mr Raddon to you—talking to you over the phone. He made an appointment for tomorrow. That's why I'm here this evening."

The Z-Man stared at him without speaking, rolling a pencil monotonously between his fingers. The sudden shattering discovery that the notorious Saint knew so much must have hit him like a blow in the stomach. Recovery was not easy. Meanwhile Simon had leisure to inspect his victim with greater care. His sight had accommodated itself to the unequal lighting, and he was able to form a fair picture of Mr Zeidelmann's appearance.

He had to acknowledge that if he had set out to feast his eyes he was doomed to be disappointed again. Mr Zeidelmann was no feast except in sheer quantity. He was grossly fat, with a great swelling belly which occupied all the space between his chair and the desk. A thick woollen muffler was bundled round his neck, and above it the Saint could catch only a glimpse of the dark beard which camouflaged the shape of his chin. Big horn-rimmed spectacles with clumsily thick rims covered his eyes, and a wide-brimmed soft hat was pulled well down over his forehead.

"You know, brother, if you're one of the curios I wouldn't want you on my mantelpiece," observed the Saint critically. "You remind me of a great, fat, over-grown slug. Only in appearance of course; for slugs are highly moral and inoffensive creatures, and their only crime is to sneak up on your lettuces at night and test their succulency. By the way, I wonder if you leave a visible trail of slime behind you wherever you go?"

"You make the mistake!" Zeidelmann said gutturally. "I nodding vot you say understand. I am not this man you say. You come here, und you insult me—"

"And call you a slug—"

"Und say I am a Z-Man, votever that iss," proceeded Mr Zeidelmann wrathfully. "I tell you, you make the mistake. You are one pig fool."

"You can't get away with it, Ariolimax Agrestis—which, believe it or not, is what Mama Slug calls Papa Slug when she wants to cut a dash," said the Saint imperturbably. "You didn't know I was such a walking encyclopedia, did you? There's no mystery about it really. You see, slug, I always make a point of knowing everything there is to be known about obnoxious vermin and pernicious germ life."

"Vill you go avay?" thundered Mr Zeidelmann.

"In a way," said the Saint, "you puzzle me. You're not particularly good, and I'm wondering where you got your Frankenstein reputation. I'm beginning to think that you're just an amateur. Blackmailers often are. But your racket isn't exactly common-or-garden black, is it? You seem to mix it with kidnapping on the side. You've hit a new angle of the game, and you've got me guessing."

"Me, too!" fumed the big man in the chair. "I, too, guess! Vot you mean I do not know."

"Oh yes, you do; and you'd better know what I mean when I tell you that Beatrice Avery is now out of your reptilian reach," said the Saint coldly. "She's safely hidden away—and so are your other intended victims."

"You are crazy mad. I haf no victims."

"You also have a large sackful of boodle tucked away somewhere, Mr Vell, and when the right time comes I'm going to dig my shovel into it." The Saint was missing none of the Z-Man's many reactions. He watched his victim's hands, his heaving stomach and his dark vicious eyes, just visible behind the big lenses. "As far as I can see you've been running your show too long, so I'm going to close it down." He pulled himself off the door and shifted closer towards the desk. "And now if you don't mind we're going to have a much more intimate look at you, as the bishop said to the actress. Take off the fur and the windows and give your face an airing."

He made a suggestive move of the hand which still rested in his pocket; and then his ears caught a faint whisper of sound behind him. He started to turn, but he was a shade too late. The door behind him was already open, and something round and hard jabbed accurately into his spine. The toneless voice of Mr Raddon spoke behind him.

"Take your hand out of your pocket and keep still."

The Saint kept still.

"This is a dirty trick, Andy," he complained. "I distinctly heard you tell Comrade Vell that you'd meet him tomorrow at the usual place. Why can't you keep your word instead of butting in like this and spoiling everything?"

He continued to keep studiously still, but he did not move his hand from his pocket. The bantering serenity of his voice had not changed in the slightest degree, and the smile on his lips was unaltered. The Z-Man, who had struggled cumbersomely to his feet, did not know that behind that blandly unruffled smile the Saint's brain was turning over like a high-speed turbine.

"Shut the door, Raddon," he said tensely. "Your gun in his back keep, und if he a muscle moves, shoot."

"Well done, slug," approved the Saint. "You sound exactly like Dennis the Dachshund."

"So, Mr Saint, your cleverness iss not so hot, yes?" Zeidelmann's voice came in a throaty purr. "There are things that even you do not know—you who knows so much about slugs. You do not know that I haf a code with Raddon for use on the telephone. 'Tomorrow' means 'today', und 'today' means 'tomorrow.' 'Yes' means 'no', und 'no' means 'yes.' Ve are careful, yes?"

"No," said the Saint. "Or should that be 'yes'? It sounds like a silly game to me. Don't you ever get muddled?"

The pressure on his spine increased.

"You talk too much," Raddon said curtly. "Take your gun out of your pocket and put it on the desk."

The Saint's eyes were twinkling blue icicles.

"Talking about guns, where did you get this one from?" he enquired. "I took one rod from you, and I've got it in my pocket at this very moment. Guns aren't so easy to pick up in London. I believe you're bluffing, Andy."

"You drivelling fool!" grated Raddon. "Do as I tell
you."

There was more than impatience and exasperation
in his voice. It was just a little too sharp to be convincing.
Simon Templar laughed almost inaudibly and took the
chance that he had to take.

"You haven't got a gun, brother," he said softly. "Have
you?"

Without warning his right heel swung back in a kick
that any mule in the full bloom of robust health would
have boasted about for weeks. Mr Raddon collected it
on his shin, and as he reeled back with a shriek of agony
the Saint spun round like a human flywheel, his arm
slamming vimfully into the other's wrist. His precaution
was unnecessary, for the object which clattered to the
floor from Raddon's hand was a harmless piece of iron
piping.

"Your ideas are too juvenile," said the Saint sadly.
"I read detective stories myself. Instead of fooling about
with that chunk of gas barrel you ought to have whacked
me on the back of the head with it."

Several other things happened immediately afterwards—one of them quite unrehearsed and unexpected.
As Raddon bumped into the wall and clawed wildly at
it to keep his balance his hand dragged over the electric
light switch to which the standard lamp was connected.
Instantly the room was plunged into inky darkness, for
there was no light out in the passage near enough to
penetrate the glass top of the door. The Saint leaped
towards the switch, his gun now snug in his fist; and as
he did so a splintering crash of glass came from the other
side of the room, and he looked round and saw an uneven patch of grey light in the blackness. He knew just
what had happened. The Z-Man, fearing that the tables
were to be turned again, had left his lieutenant to his

fate and charged desperately into the window, taking blind and glass and broken frame with him. Mr Zeidelmann was nothing if not thorough.

The Saint dashed for the window, and one of his feet got caught in the flex of the table lamp and almost tripped him. It was only a brief delay, but that was all the Z-Man needed. When Simon dived through the window into the narrow alley which ran along the rear of the building he caught a glimpse of a bulky, lumbering figure streaking away beneath a solitary lamp at the far corner. Considering Mr Zeidelmann's load of superfluous flesh, he certainly knew how to sprint. The Saint ran to the end of the alley and found himself in a dingy side street. A little way from this was a main road, with buses and other heavy traffic. The Z-Man had vanished into the anonymity of London's millions.

Simon was not surprised to find Mr Otto Zeidelmann's office empty when he got back. Nobody seemed to have noticed the crash of glass, if there was anyone left in the building to notice it; and Mr Raddon had clearly wasted no time in taking advantage of his opportunity. The Saint was not disturbed about that—he had already had all that he wanted from Comrade Raddon in a business way, and an extension of their acquaintance along social lines was something that the Saint could hardly see as a pleasure without which life would be merely a succession of empty hours.

He retrieved his knife from the arm of the chair and made a quick search of the office. As he had anticipated, every drawer of the desk was empty except the middle one, which contained a loaded revolver of ancient design. It was obvious that the Z-Man used the office only for a base of communications when his assistants were on the job. He was too clever to have any hand in the actual operations, but he could be reached by telephone if necessary. And after this, Simon reflected ruefully, he would certainly find himself a new address and telephone number. . . . The visit hadn't been anything like as profitable as he had hoped it would be, but it had been fun while it lasted. And at least, in spite of disguises, he would have some slight chance of recognizing Mr Zeidelmann when they met again. The Saint's mind always turned optimistically towards the boundless possibilities of the future. He wondered how Patricia was getting on with her share of the campaign.

VII

Patricia Holm had had little or no difficulty in inducing Beatrice Avery to leave her apartment and go down to the big limousine with Hoppy Uniatz at the wheel which waited outside. With that calm realism which was peculiarly her own she had described her recent adventure, and the film actress had come to the obvious conclusion that Parkside Court was the unhealthiest spot in London. Perhaps she had been close to that conclusion even before that, for since Patricia's last visit she had had time to reconsider the Saint's offer.

"I asked for it, in a way," said Patricia as the car raced towards Piccadilly. "I took advantage of my superficial resemblance to you to gain admission to your flat, and when the Z-Man's agents saw me come out they made the same mistake as your bodyguard."

"Supposing it had really been me?" said Beatrice Avery with a shudder. "I shouldn't have had the Saint to help me."

"Well, you've got him now," said Patricia. "So you can stop worrying. The Saint's after the Z-Man, and that means that the Z-Man will have so much on his mind that he won't have time to think about you."

"But why are we going to Scotland?"

"We're not going to Scotland."

"When we were on our way out you said you always preferred to motor to Scotland at night because the roads were clearer—"

"That was just for the benefit of the commissionaire," Patricia explained.

The car stopped outside a handsome new apartment house in Berkeley Square. Patricia went up to Irene Cromwell's extravagant flat. The exotic star of Pyramid Pictures was not in.

"I think she had better be," said Patricia to the scared-looking maid who had answered the door. "Tell her that Miss Holm, of the Special Branch, Scotland Yard, wishes to see her on a matter which affects her personal safety."

The maid, duly impressed, discovered that her mistress was in after all. She left Patricia in the little hall for only a minute and then ushered her into a gorgeous boudoir which only a five-hundred-pound-a-week film star could dream of maintaining. Irene Cromwell looked surprisingly frail and timid, wrapped in a trailing, feather-trimmed chiffon negligee.

"You are from Scotland Yard?" she asked, her eyes round and big.

"I don't want to beat about the bush," replied Patricia, her manner brisk and efficient. "It has come to our knowledge at Scotland Yard that the Z-Man is active again. . . ."

"The Z-Man!" breathed the other girl, turning deathly pale.

"Oh yes, we know all about him, and we think it would be wise to transfer you to a place of safety," continued Patricia imperturbably. "I have an official car waiting outside. Miss Beatrice Avery, whom you probably know, is in the car already. You will also be accompanied, I hope, by Miss Sheila Ireland."

The startled actress opened her eyes even wider.

"But where are we going? I've got a dinner engagement—"

"Ireland," answered Patricia, without batting an eyelid. "We have everything arranged with the Free State authorities. Ireland is within a comparatively few hours and yet sufficiently remote for our purpose. You see, Miss Cromwell, it is of vital importance that Scotland Yard should be left with a clear field. While this organization is being cleaned up you are in grave danger."

Irene Cromwell took less than a minute to make up her mind. In fact she regarded Patricia's suggestion as a police order; and so thoroughly had the urgency of the matter impressed itself on her mind that she was ready, with two packed suitcases, within the incredible space of twenty minutes.

Beatrice Avery had been given her cue, and she kept up the deception as the limousine rolled smoothly off towards Kensington. But very little was said. Irene Cromwell sat back in her corner, huddled in her furs, apparently fascinated by the very official-looking cap which reposed on the unprepossessing head of Mr Uniatz.

Exactly the same procedure was followed in Sheila Ireland's dainty home—and again Patricia got away with it. The blonde Venus of Summit Pictures was successfully lured out into the waiting car; and any doubts she might have entertained were dispelled when she saw Beatrice Avery and Irene Cromwell. An impression was left behind that Miss Ireland was bound for a remote spot in the Welsh mountains.

At Patricia's request further discussion of the subject that was uppermost in all their minds was tacitly postponed. The limousine now started off in real earnest, leaving London behind and speeding through the night in the direction of Kingston. Their actual destination was Weybridge, less than twenty miles to the southwest.

Simon Templar's house on St George's Hill was not easily found at night, but Hoppy Uniatz knew every inch of that aristocratic neighbourhood with its nameless roads and its discreetly hidden residences which were far too exclusive to be demeaned by ordinary numbers. The passengers in the car caught vague glimpses of pine trees and silver birches which rose from the rolling banks of rhododendrons and bracken.

There were bright lights in the windows as the limousine came to a standstill outside the front door; and a man with a loose walrus moustache and a curious strutting limp came out on the step.

"Here we are, Orace," said Patricia as she got out.

"Yer lyte," replied Orace unemotionally.

He took charge of the suitcases and showed no surprise at seeing three of the prettiest girls in England follow Patricia out of the car. If they had been three performing kangaroos he wouldn't even blinked. Years of employment in Simon Templar's service had deprived him of any quality of surprise he might have once possessed.

"Dinner narf a minnit," he said when they were in the hall, and stumped off to his own quarters.

"He means it too," smiled Patricia. "But for once Orace and the dinner must be kept waiting."

She led them into the living room and looked from Irene Cromwell to Sheila Ireland with quiet calmness. Mr Uniatz, who had helped to carry the bags in, licked his lips and gazed longingly at the cocktail cabinet, where liquor was always to be found in plenty and in great variety. But he caught Patricia's warning eye, and he knew that the time for refreshment had not yet come.

His impersonation of a police officer was no longer important, but Patricia Holm felt that the sudden shock of Mr Uniatz's speech would be lessened if she explained certain other things to her guests beforehand.

"You'll forgive me, I hope, for practising a small deception," she said, in her forthright way. "Miss Avery knows that I'm not really connected with Scotland Yard. I am Patricia Holm, and this house belongs to Simon Templar."

"You mean—the Saint?" asked Irene with a little quiver of excitement and incredulity.

"The Saint is out to get the Z-Man, and before he could let himself go he had to be sure that he wouldn't be placing any of you in danger," Patricia went on. "I took the risk of lying to you in London because it was too urgent to go into explanations. But before we go any farther I want to tell you that you're free to go whenever you please. This very minute if you like. Any one of you or all three of you can go if you want to. You haven't been kidnapped. The car is ready to take you back to London. But if you're wise you'll stay here. I'll tell you why."

Irene and Sheila, bewildered at first, began to understand as she went on; and Beatrice Avery contributed some heartfelt persuasions of her own. And while they talked the subtle atmosphere of peace and security with which the Saint had invested the house began to add its charm to the other arguments. The girls looked at each other and then at the less comforting dark outside. . . .

"Well, you've been very frank about it, Miss Holm," said Irene Cromwell at length. "I'm willing to stay if you think it would help. But the studio—"

"You can phone them in the morning and say you've been taken ill."

"But why are we safer here than in London?" asked Sheila.

Patricia smiled.

"With Orace and Hoppy Uniatz to look after us we can make faces at a dozen Z-Men," she replied confidently. "Also nobody except yourselves knows where you are. And this house isn't quite as innocent as it looks. It has all sorts of surprises for people who try to crash the gate. Now suppose we have a cocktail."

Mr Uniatz drew a deep breath.

"Say, ain't dat an idea?" he asked of the assembled company with the enthusiasm of an alchemist who has just heard of the elixir of life. "Dat 'll make everyt'ing okay."

Orace was serving the second course of dinner when he cocked his head on one side and listened. Patricia, too, had heard the familiar drone of the Hirondel.

"It's 'im," remarked Orace ominously. "And abaht time too. 'E'll get some cold soup."

VIII

Chief Inspector Teal was out of his office when Raddon's telephone call came through to Scotland Yard. Consequently another officer went to Parkside Court, purely as a matter of routine, to make a few discreet enquiries. All he learned was that Beatrice Avery had left for Scotland and that she had been accompanied by her sister. It seemed, therefore, that the telephone call was true to type—in other words merely another of those pointless practical jokes which regularly add to the tribulations of the C.I.D.

Mr Teal, when he heard about it, was not so sure.

It is a matter of record that he set off to Parkside Court without a minute's delay to make some enquiries of his own; and they were not so discreet. He cross-examined the hall porter and the commissionaire and the elevator boy until they were in momentary expectation of being dumped into a Black Maria and shot off to the cells. Mr Teal was definitely suspicious because when he had interviewed Beatrice Avery that afternoon she had definitely assured him that she had no intention of leaving London. And now, apparently, she had gone off to Scotland.

"Why Scotland?" demanded Mr Teal, turning his baby blue eyes smoulderingly on the commissionaire.

"She didn't tell me she was going to Scotland," said the man. "But I heard her sister saying that they'd have a nice clear run—"

"How do you know it was her sister?"

"That private detective chap who was here told me so," said the commissionaire. "As soon as they'd gone he went off duty. Miss Avery's maid went home too. The flat's empty."

From the description supplied by the commissionaire and the elevator boy Mr Teal had no difficulty in recognizing Patricia Holm. His worst suspicions were strengthened when the commissionaire proffered the additional information that the limousine which had waited outside had been driven by a large man with a face which had the appearance of having once been run over by a traction engine and afterwards left in the hands of an amateur face-lifter.

"The Holm girl and Uniatz!" raged Mr Teal, champing viciously on his flavourless spearmint. "It's as clear as daylight! They came here as openly as a couple of innocent schoolchildren and got her away with some fairy tale. I'll bet it was the Saint himself who rang up the Yard—just to get my goat!"

These remarks he addressed to himself as he paced

up and down the luxuriously carpeted foyer. The monumental conviction was growing within him, and rapidly assuming the size of the Arc de Triomphe, that the Saint had made every variety of fool of him in the early afternoon.

Simon Templar was the Z-Man. Mr Teal's grey matter was flowing like molten lava. The Saint had spotted Sergeant Barrow at the Dorchester, and on the off-chance that Barrow had spotted him he had thought it advisable to shoot back the package of money to Beatrice Avery so that he could clear himself. Whatever hold he had on her had been enough to force her to lie on the telephone. Then, to keep her quiet, he had kidnapped her. . . . It was like the Saint's devilish sense of humour to ring up. . . . There wasn't any real proof. . . . But if he could find Beatrice Avery in the Saint's hands there would be enough evidence to put him away for keeps, the detective told himself to the accompaniment of an imaginary fanfare of triumphal trumpets. It would be the last time that the Saint would pull a long nose at the majesty of the law. . . .

Seething and sizzling like a firework about to go off, Mr Teal realized that he was wasting time at Parkside Court. He plunged into the police car which had brought him, and was driven to Cornwall House. He guessed that this would be a further waste of time, but the visit had to be made. He was right. Not only did Sam Outrell coldly inform him that the Saint was away, but he used a passkey to show him the empty flat. Fuming and expectorating a devitalized lump of chicle onto the sidewalk for the unwary to step on, he climbed into his car again and this time told the driver to go to Abbot's Yard in Chelsea. It was well known that the Saint owned a studio in this modernized slum.

"We might as well try it," Teal said grimly. "Ten to

one they've taken the girl out of London, but it would be just like the Saint's blasted nerve to hold her here right under our very noses."

Again his fears were confirmed. Twenty-six Abbot's Yard was in the same condition as Mother Hubbard's cupboard; and enquiries among the near-artist neighbours elicited the information that the Saint had not been seen for weeks.

Mr Teal was so exasperated that he nearly inserted the next slice of spearmint into his mouth without removing the pink wrapper; but on the intellectual side his grey matter was not quite so white hot now and therefore was slightly more efficient. He was certain of one thing: the Saint had not taken Beatrice Avery to Scotland. After years of experience of Simon Templar's methods Mr Teal easily guessed that Patricia Holm's reference to Scotland had very much the fishy smell of a red herring.

"Not much good looking for him, is it, sir?" asked the driver of the police car depressingly.

"No; let's sit down on the curb and play shove-ha'penny," retorted Mr Teal with searing sarcasm.

"I mean, sir, the Saint's got all sorts of hideouts," said the man. "There's no telling—"

"I've long since come to the conclusion that most of these stories of the Saint are pure legend," said Mr Teal with a real flash of intelligence. "In nine cases out of ten he remains in full view and just dares us to do our worst. One of these days he's going to dare us once too often. Perhaps this is the day," he added hopefully. "Anyhow, let's get going."

"Where to, sir?"

"We know he's got a place at Weybridge, so we might as well run down and have a look at it," replied Mr Teal, climbing into the car. "We'll try every place we know until we find him."

The more he thought of his recent interview with the Saint, the more he reviewed the subsequent happenings, the higher became his dudgeon. In everything except outward appearance Chief Inspector Teal was exactly like a fire-breathing dragon as he sat in the back of the car, asking the driver why he had left the engine behind and what was the blank-blank idea of driving with the brakes full on.

However, in spite of his unsympathetic comments the journey was accomplished in remarkably good time, and a gleam of hope appeared in Mr Teal's overheated blue eyes when he saw lights gleaming from the windows of Simon Templar's house on St George's Hill. In answer to his thunderous knock and insistent ringing the door was opened by Orace, who inspected him with undisguised disfavour.

"Oh, it's you, is it?" said Orace witheringly.

"Is Templar here?" roared Mr Teal.

"Is 'oo 'ere? If you mean *Mister* Templar—"

"I mean Mr Templar!" said the detective chokingly. "Is Mr Templar here?"

"Oo wants ter know?"

"I want to know!" bellowed Mr Teal, his spleen surging out of him like a discharge of poison gas. "Stand out of the way, my man. I'm coming in—"

"Like 'ell you are," Orace said stolidly. "Back door fer you, my man. The idear!"

At this point of the proceedings Simon Templar, resplendent in tuxedo and soft silk shirt, materialized into the picture. The living-room door was half open, and the Saint had an idea that the dialogue would soon become blue around the edges and unfit for the shell-like ears of his guests.

"All right, Orace," he said breezily. "Walk right in,

Claud Eustace. What brings you into the wilds this evening? Not that I wasn't expecting you—"

"Oh, you were expecting me, were you?" broke in Mr Teal, forcing the words past his strained throttle with some difficulty. "Well, I hope you're glad to be right. You've been just a little too smart since I saw you this afternoon. Now I know damned well you *are* the Z-Man!"

"In that case, dear heart, there must be two Z-Men," answered the Saint accommodatingly. "Isn't it amazing how the little fellows breed? I'm glad you're here, Claud. There's something I want you to do. It'll interest you to know that I had quite a chat with the original Z-Man this evening—"

"When I want to listen to any more of that I'll let you know," Teal said massively. "Just now I'm going to be busy. I have reason to believe that you kidnapped Miss Beatrice Avery from her apartment in Parkside Court this evening, and I'm not going to leave this house until I've searched it—and you might as well know that I haven't got a warrant."

"But why search the house, dear old fungus?" Simon protested reasonably. "Kidnapping is a hard word, and I resent it. But I'm willing to make allowances for your blood pressure. At the rate the red corpuscles are being pumped through that lump of petrified wood you wear your hat on the poor thing must be feeling the strain. Have I denied that Miss Avery is under this roof? She came down with Patricia a little more than an hour ago, and we're just having our coffee."

Mr Teal gulped, and his chewing gum slithered to the back of his mouth, played hide-and-seek with his tonsils and finally slid into his gullet before he could recover it.

"What!" His voice was like a pinpricked carnival balloon. "You admit you've got her here? You admit you're the Z-Man? Then by God—"

"My poor boob," said the Saint sympathetically, "I haven't admitted anything of the sort. I merely said that Miss Avery was having dinner with me. If that makes me the Z-Man it makes you the Grand Lama of Tibet. Miss Avery is a friend of Pat's, and we've got a couple of other good-looking girls here too. We're making a collection of them. If you'll promise to behave yourself I'll take you in and let you look at them."

He turned back into the living room, and Mr Teal followed him with the beginnings of a new vacuum pumping itself out from under his belt. Somehow it was going to be done again—the awful certainty of it made Mr Teal feel physically sick. He had a wild desire to turn back to his car and drive away to the end of the earth and forget that he had ever seen Scotland Yard, but he had to drag himself on, like a condemned man walking to the scaffold.

He stood in the doorway with his hands clasped tightly on his belt and stared around at the four eye-filling sirens who reclined in armchairs around the fire. Patricia Holm and Beatrice Avery he knew; but his heavy eyelids nearly disappeared into the back of his head when he heard the names of Irene Cromwell and Sheila Ireland. And the worst of it was that they all looked perfectly happy. They didn't leap up with shrill cries of joy and greet him as their deliverer. They studied him with the detached curiosity of surgeons inspecting a new kind of tumour revealed by an operation.

Mr Teal grunted his acknowledgment of the introductions and stood glaring desperately at Beatrice Avery.

"I've got one thing to ask you, Miss Avery," he said with a hideous presentiment of what the answer would be. "Did you come here entirely of your own free will?"

"I think that's a very unkind thing to ask, Mr Teal," she answered sweetly. "It's unkind to me, since it implies that I'm weak minded; and it's unkind to Mr Templar—"

"I want to be unkind to Mr Templar!" Teal stated homicidally. "If there is any kind of threat being held over you, Miss Avery, I give you my word that so long as I'm here—"

"Of course there isn't any threat," she said. "How ridiculous! What do you think Mr Templar is—a sort of Bluebeard?"

Mr Teal didn't dare to say what he thought Mr Templar was. But he knew that Beatrice Avery would give him no help. There was nothing about her that gave the slightest hint of fear or anxiety. However accomplished an actress she might be, he knew that she could never have acted like that under compulsion. What other supernatural means the Saint had taken to silence her, Mr Teal couldn't imagine; but he knew that it was hopeless to fight them.

He pulled himself miserably together.

"I don't think I need bother you with any more questions, Miss Avery," he said brusquely.

He went out of the room very much like a beaten dog, and if he had had a tail it would have been hanging between his legs. The Saint followed him out, closed the door and lighted a fresh cigarette.

"Cheer up, Claud," he said kindly. "You've got over these things before, and you'll get over it again. Look me squarely in the eye and tell me you're sorry I'm not the Z-Man, and I'll spread you all over the hall in a mass of squashy pulp."

The detective looked at him for a long time.

"Damn it, Saint, you've got me," he growled sheepishly. "You know how much I want to get my hands on you, but I'd still be glad if you weren't the Z-Man."

"Then why not be glad?"

"I think I'm getting some more ideas now," Teal went on, flashing the Saint a glance which was very far from sleepy. "Miss Avery—Miss Cromwell—Miss Ireland. Top-line film stars, every one. Let me make another guess. Those girls are the Z-Man's intended victims; and if you aren't the Z-Man yourself you've brought them here so that they'll be safe while you go after him."

"You must have been eating a lot of fish and spinach," said the Saint respectfully. "Your ideas are improving every minute—except for one minor detail. I've been out after the Z-Man already, I've met him, and we had quite an interesting five minutes."

Mr Teal, who had just rolled up a fresh slice of spearmint with his tongue like a miniature piece of music, shook his head sceptically.

"Just because I'll believe you up to a point—"

"Would I lie to you, Claud?" asked the Saint. "Have I ever told you anything but the truth? Listen, brother, I don't know much about the Z-Man, but I can tell you this. Until this evening he has been known as Mr Otto Zeidelmann, and he's large and fat and has a black beard and wears horn-rimmed glasses and speaks with a phony German accent. He has been using an office in Bryerby House, Victoria, for his business address; but you needn't trouble to look for him there, because I don't think he likes the place so much now. And I doubt if his appearance in ordinary life is anything like my description. But that's where I saw him, and that's what he looked like to me."

Mr Teal opened his mouth, but words failed him.

"And here's a gun," Simon went on, taking something wrapped in a silk handkerchief from his pocket. "It's one of my own, but I fooled a gentleman who goes by the name of Raddon into making a grab for it, and you ought to find a fair sample of his fingerprints. Get Records to look them up, will you? I have an idea it's what you professionals call a Clue. I'll drop into your office in the morning and get your report. Has that percolated?"

"Yes," replied Mr Teal, taking the gun and putting it carefully away. "But I'm damned if I get the rest. Is this another of your tricks, or are you playing the game for once? We've been trying to get a line on the Z-Man for months—"

"And I heard of him for the first time today," murmured the Saint with a smile. "You can call it luck if you like, but most of it's due to the fact that I'm not festooned with red tape until I look like a Bolshevik Egyptian mummy. Having a free and unfettered hand is a great help. It might even help you to solve a mystery sometimes—but I'm not so sure about that."

"Well, what are you getting out of it?" asked Mr Teal with reasonable curiosity. "If you think I'm going to believe that you're doing this for fun—"

"Maybe I might persuade the Z-Man to contribute towards my old age pension," Simon admitted meditatively, as though the idea had just occurred to him. "But it's still a lot of fun. And if you get his body, dead or alive, you ought to be satisfied. Don't you think you're asking rather a lot of questions?"

Mr Teal did, but he couldn't help it. His mind would never be at ease about anything so long as he knew that the Saint was busy. He stared resentfully at the smiling man in front of him and wondered if he was still only being hoodwinked again.

"I've got to get back to town," he said curtly. "I'm sorry about the misunderstanding. But who the devil *did* phone that message through to the Yard?"

"That was Comrade Raddon, whose fingerprints are

carefully preserved on that gun in your pocket," Simon replied. "I expect he thought it was a bright idea. Now run along home and play with your toys."

Mr Teal hitched his coat round.

"I'm going," he said, fighting a losing battle with the new crop of gnawing suspicions that were springing up all over the well-fertilized tracts of his unhappy mind. "But get this. If you still think you're putting anything over on me—"

"I know," said the Saint. "I needn't think I can get away with it. How empty the days would be if I couldn't hear that dear old litany! I think I could recite it in my sleep. Come again, Claud, and we'll have some new grey hairs for you." He opened the front door and steered the detective affectionately down the steps. "Take care of Mr Teal, George," he said to the police driver who still sat at the wheel of the car. "He isn't feeling very strong just now."

He patted the detective's bowler hat well down over his ears and went back into the house.

IX

Back in the living room the Saint's air of leisured badinage fell off him like a cloak. He draped himself on the mantelpiece with a cigarette tilting from his mouth and a drink in his hand and started to ask questions. He had a lot to ask.

They were not easy questions, and the answers were mostly vague and unsatisfactory. The subject of the Z-Man was not one that seemed to encourage conversation; but Simon Templar had a knack of his own of making people talk, and what he did learn was significant enough. Two or three months earlier Mercia Landon, dancing and singing star of Atlantic Studios, had been working in the final sequences of a new supermusical when for no apparent reason she had had a breakdown. All work on the production was held up, the overhead mounted perilously, and finally the picture had to be shelved. It was rumoured that Mercia was being threatened by a blackmailer, but nobody knew anything for certain. And then one morning she was found dead in her apartment from the conventional overdose of veronal.

"Accidental death," said the coroner's jury, since there was no evidence to show that the overdose had been deliberately taken; but those "in the know"—people on the inside of the screen world—knew perfectly well that Mercia Landon had taken her own life. And for a good and sufficient reason. Although she was only twenty-two and in perfect health, she had known that her screen career was finished. For when her maid found her there was a deep and jagged cut on her face in the rough zigzag shape of a Z. The upper line crossed her eyebrows, the diagonal crossed her nose, and the lower horizontal gashed her mouth almost from ear to ear. No amount of plastic surgery, no miracles of skin grafting could ever have restored the famous modelling of her face or made it possible for her to smile again that quick sunny smile that had been reflected from a million screens.

"Nobody ever knew who Mercia met that night or even where she went," said Sheila Ireland, her slim white fingers nervously twisting her empty cigarette holder. "I suppose they took her away like—like they thought they were taking Beatrice. Nobody could have blackmailed Mercia. She never had any affairs, and everybody loved her. And she just laughed at the idea of being kidnapped—here in England. When they started demanding money she just laughed at it. She wouldn't even go to the police. All anybody knows about this is that she once said to her maid: 'That idiotic Z-Man who keeps phoning must be an escaped lunatic.' And then—" She shivered. "Since then we've all been terrified."

"It's an old racket with a new twist," said the Saint. "The ordinary blackmailer has something on his victim. The Z-Man has nothing—except the threat that he'll disfigure them and ruin their screen careers if they don't come across. I seem to remember that some other actress recently had a nervous breakdown, exactly like Mercia Landon. The picture she was in was shelved, too, and it's still shelved. She went to Italy to recuperate. I take it that she was victim number two. She was threatened, she lost her nerve, and she paid. She saved her good looks, but her bank balance wasn't big enough to go on paying. So Beatrice is probably victim number three."

The girl shuddered.

"I know I am," she said. "During the last three weeks I've had three telephone calls—always in a thick, guttural, foreign sort of voice, asking me for ten tousand pounds. I was told to lunch at the Dorchester, and if I saw that the knives and forks formed the letter Z I was to have my lunch and then leave the package of money under my napkin. And he said if I went to the police or anything they'd know about it, and they'd do the same to me as they did to Mercia without giving me another chance to pay. . . . Today was my last chance, and when I saw the knives and forks in the shape of a Z I think I lost my nerve. When you came to my table, Mr Templar, I thought you must be the man who was to take the money. I hardly knew what I was doing—"

"Take a look at that cunning, will you, Pat?" said the Saint. "It's a million to one that his victim won't go to the police; but he's even ready for that millionth chance. He's ready to pick up the money as soon as the girl has left the table; disguised as a gentleman, he's sitting there all the time, and as he walks past the table he collars the package. And he's got his alibi if the police should be watching and pick him up. He happened to see the young lady had left something, and he was going to hand it over to the manager. No proof at all that he's the man they're really after. It also implies that he must be some-body with a name and reputation as clean as an unsettled snowflake and as far above suspicion as the strato-sphere. . . . But who was it? There was a whole raft of people at the Dorchester, and I can't remember all of them—unless it was good old Sergeant Barrow."

"If the Z-Man was in the Dorchester today he must have seen your knightly behaviour," said Patricia thoughtfully. "And he must have seen you pocket Bea-trice's last week's salary."

"But he didn't know who I was, and I expect he beetled off as soon as he saw that something had come ungummed," said the Saint, stubbing the end of his cig-arette into an ash tray and lighting a fresh one. He turned. "What about the picture you're working on now, Bea-trice? I'll make a guess that it's nearly finished, and if anything happened to you now the whole schedule would be shot to hell."

She nodded.

"It would be—and so should I. My contract doesn't entitle me to a penny if I don't complete the picture. That's why—"

She broke off helplessly.

Simon went to bed with plenty to think about. The Z-Man's plan of campaign was practically foolproof. Film stars are able to command colossal salaries for their good looks as well as their ability to act—sometimes even more so. All three of his guests were in the twenty-thousand-pounds-a-year class; they were young, with the hope of many more years of stardom ahead of them. Obviously it would be better for them to pay half a year's salary to the Z-Man rather than suffer the ghastly disfigurement that had been inflicted on Mercia Landon; for then they would lose not only half a year's salary but all their salaries for all the years to come.

The film world still didn't really know what was happening. Beatrice Avery had been afraid to tell even her employers about the threats she had received, for fear that the Z-Man would promptly carry out his hideous promise. Irene Cromwell and Sheila Ireland had each received one message from the Z-Man and had been similarly terrorized to silence. Only Patricia's blunt statement that the Saint had found their photographs in Raddon's pocket had made them unseal their lips after she had got them to St George's Hill.

Simon could well understand why he had never heard of the Z-Man before. Even in the film world the name was only rumoured, and then rumoured with scepticism. These three girls were the only ones who *knew,* apart from Mercia Landon, who was dead, and the actress who had fled to Italy.

For once in his life he spent a restless night, impatient for the chance of further developments the next day; and he walked into Chief Inspector Teal's office at what was for him the fantastic hour of eleven o'clock in the morning.

"I thought you never got up before the streets were aired," said the detective.

"I put on some woolly underwear this morning and chanced it," said the Saint briefly. "What do you know?"

Mr Teal drew a memorandum towards him.

"We've checked up on that address you gave me. I think you're right, Saint. There's no such person as Otto Zeidelmann. It's just a name. He's had the office about three or four months."

"His occupation dates from about the time Mercia Landon died," said Simon, nodding. "Anything else?"

"He never went there in the daytime apparently," answered the detective. "Always after dark. Hardly anybody can remember seeing him. The postman can't remember delivering any letters, and we didn't find a fingerprint anywhere."

"You wouldn't," said the Saint. "A wily bird like him would be just as likely to walk about naked as go out without his gloves. But talking about fingerprints, what's the report on that gun?—which, by the way, is mine."

Mr Teal opened a drawer, produced the automatic and pushed it across the desk. Chewing rhythmically, he also handed the Saint a card on which were full face and profile photographs of one Nathan Everill.

"Know him?"

"My old college chum, Andy Gump—otherwise known as Mr Raddon," said the Saint at once. "So he has got a police record. I thought as much. What do we know about him?"

"Not very much. He's not one of the regulars." Teal consulted his memorandum, although he probably knew it by heart already. "He's only been through our hands once, and that was in 1933. From 1928 to 1933 he was private secretary to Hubert Sentinel, the film producer, and then he started making copies of Mr Sentinel's signature and writing them on Mr Sentinel's cheques. One day Mr Sentinel noticed something wrong with his bank balance, and when he went to ask his secretary about it his secretary was on his way to Dover. He was sent up for three years."

"What's he been doing since he came out?"

"He reported in the usual way, and as far as we knew he was going quite straight," replied Mr Teal. "He was doing some free-lance writing, I think. We've lost track of him during the last five or six months—"

"He's got a new job—as the Z-Man's assistant," said the Saint. "And, by the Lord, he's the very man for it! He knows the inside of the film business, and he must hate every kind of screen personality, from producers downwards, like nobody's business. It's a perfect setup. . . . Have you seen Sentinel?"

"I'm seeing him this afternoon—he probably knows a lot more about Everill than we do. But you aren't usually interested in the small fry, are you?"

"When the small fry is in the shape of a sprat, yes," answered the Saint, rising elegantly to his feet. "You see, Claud, old dear, there might be a mackerel cruising about in the neighbouring waters. . . . That's a good idea of yours. I think I'll push along and see Comrade Sentinel myself."

The detective's jaw dropped.

"Hey, wait a minute!" he yapped. "You can't—"

"Can't I?" drawled the Saint with his head round the door. "And what sort of a crime is it to go and have a chat with a film producer? Maybe my face is the face the world has been waiting for."

He was gone before Teal could think of a reply.

Mr Hubert Sentinel, the grand panjandrum of Sentinel Films, was not an aristocrat by birth or even a Conservative by conviction; but even he might have been slightly upset if he had heard himself referred to as "Comrade Sentinel." For he was considered a coming man in the British film industry, and obtaining an entry into his presence was about as easy as getting into Hitler's mountain chalet with one fist clenched and a red flag in the other.

But the Saint accomplished the apparently impossible at the first attempt. He simply enclosed his card in

a sealed envelope with a request that it should be immediately delivered to Mr Sentinel, and he waited exactly
two minutes.

Mr Sentinel was in conference. He took one look at
the card, and during the next half minute one matinée
idol, one prominent author, two script writers, a famous
director and a covey of yes-men were swept out of the
office like leaves before an autumn gale. When Simon
Templar was admitted Mr Hubert Sentinel was alone,
and Mr Sentinel was looking at the back of the Saint's
card. On it were pencilled the words: *Re the Z-Man*.

"Take a pew, Mr Templar," he said, pushing forward
a cigar box and inspecting his visitor out of bright and
observant eyes. "I've heard about you of course."

"Who hasn't?" murmured the Saint modestly.

He accepted a cigar, carefully clipped the end, lighted
it and emitted a fragrant cloud of blue smoke. It was
merely an example of that theatrical timing which so
pleased the Saint's heart. Sentinel waited restively, turning a pencil between his fingers. He was a thin bald-
headed man with a birdlike face and an air of inexhaus-
tible nervous vitality.

"If it had been anyone else I should have thought it
was some crank with a bee in his bonnet," he said. "We
get a lot of them around here. But you—Are you going
to tell me that there's anything in these rumours?"

"There's everything in them,"said the Saint deliberately. "They happen to be true. The Z-Man is as real a
person as you are."

The producer stared at him.

"But why do you come to me?"

"For the very important reason that you once employed a man named Nathan Everill," answered the Saint
directly. "I'm hoping you'll be able to tell me something
useful about him."

"Good God, you're not suggesting that Everill is the Z-Man, are you?" asked the other incredulously. "He's such a poor specimen—a chinless, weak-minded fool—"

"But you employed him as your secretary for five years."

"That's true," confessed Sentinel hesitantly. "He was efficient enough—too damned efficient, as a matter of fact. But he always had a weak streak in him, and it came out in the end. He forged my name to some cheques—perhaps you know about that. . . . But Everill! It doesn't seem possible—"

The Saint shook his head.

"I didn't say he *was* the Z-Man. But I know that he's very closely connected with him. So if you can help me to locate Everill you'll probably help me to get to close quarters with the Z-Man himself. And he interests me a lot."

"If you can get him, Templar, you'll not only earn my gratitude, but the gratitude of the whole film business," said Hubert Sentinel, rising to his feet and pacing up and down with undisguised agitation. "If he's a real person at least that gives us something to fight. Up to now he's just been a name that people have tried to stick onto something they couldn't explain any other way. But when we see our stars having mysterious breakdowns just when pictures are in their last scenes—getting hysterical over something you can't make them talk about—well, we have to put it down to something."

"Then you've had trouble yourself?"

"I don't know whether it's a coincidence or not," replied Sentinel carefully. "I'll only say that my production of *Vanity Fair* is held up while Mary Donne is recovering from a slight indisposition. She has said nothing to me, and I have said nothing to her. But that doesn't prevent me from thinking. As for the rest, Mr Templar,

I believe I can tell you a great deal about Everill." He sat down again and rubbed his chin in earnest concentration. "You know, I've got some ideas of my own about the Z-Man. Can you tell me just what your interest in him is?"

"I have various interests," said the Saint, leaning back and making a series of perfect smoke rings. "The Z-Man must have collected a fair amount of boodle already, and that's always interesting. I take it that if I got rid of him nobody would mind me helping myself to a reward. And then I don't like his line of business. I think it would be rather a good idea if he was put out of the way—for keeps."

"Unless he puts *you* out of the way first," suggested the producer grimly. "If he's the sort of man he seems to be—"

The Saint shrugged.

"That's all in the game."

The other smiled appreciatively.

"I sincerely hope it won't be in your game," he said. "As for Everill—what do you want to know?"

"Anything you can remember. Anything that might give me a lead. What his tastes are—his amusements—his favourite haunts—his habits—why he started forging cheques—"

"Well, I suppose he's an extravagant little devil—wants to live like a rich playboy and so on. I suppose that's why he had to increase his income. He was trying to run one of my actresses, and he couldn't keep pace with her. She had a big future ahead of her, and she knew it—"

It was as if the Saint's ears had closed up suddenly, so that he scarcely heard any more. All his senses seemed to have been arrested except the sense of sight, and that one filled his brain to the exclusion of everything else.

He was staring at Hubert Sentinel's hands, watching the thin nervous fingers twiddling the pencil they held—and remembering another pair of hands. . . .

The astounding import of it drummed through his head like the thunder of mighty waterfalls. It jeered at his credulity, and yet he knew that he must be right. It all fitted in—even if the revelation made him feel as if his mind had been hauled loose from its moorings. He sat in a kind of daze until a knock on the door brought him back to life.

Sentinel's secretary put her head in the door.

"Chief Inspector Teal is here, Mr Sentinel," she said.

"Oh yes." Sentinel stopped in the middle of a sentence. He explained: "Mr Teal made an appointment with me—is he interested in Everill too?"

"Very much," said the Saint. "In fact I was stealing a march on him. If there's any other way I can go out—"

Sentinel stood up.

"Of course—my secretary will show you. I wish we could have a longer talk, Mr Templar. The police are admirable in their way, but in a situation like this—" He seemed to come to a snap decision. "Look here, could you dine with me tonight?"

"I'd be delighted," said the Saint thoughtfully.

"That's splendid. And then we can go into this thoroughly without any interruptions." Sentinel held out his hand. "Will you come back here at six? I'll drive you out myself—I live out at Bushey Park."

Simon nodded.

"I'll be here," he said.

He went back to Cornwall House with his head still buzzing; and for a long time he paced up and down the living room, smoking an interminable chain of cigarettes and scattering a trail of ash behind him on the carpet. At lunchtime he called Patricia.

"I've met a bird called Hubert Sentinel, and I think I know who the Z-Man is," he said. "I'm having dinner with him tonight."

He heard her gasp of amazement.

"But, boy, you can't—"

"Listen," he said. "You and Hoppy are going to be busy. I've got a lot more for you."

He talked for ten minutes that left her stunned and gave her comprehensive instructions.

Six o'clock was striking when he re-entered Sentinel's office, and the producer took down his hat at once. A large Rolls-Royce was parked outside the studio, and Sentinel himself took the wheel.

"How did you get on with Scotland Yard?" Simon enquired as they purred through the gates.

Sentinel shifted his cigar.

"I had to give him a certain amount of information, but I didn't say anything about your visit. I noticed that he kept looking at the cigarettes in the ash tray, though, so perhaps he was trying to spot your brand."

"Poor old Claud," said the Saint. "He still keeps on reading Sherlock Holmes!"

Little more was said on the swift northward run, but the Saint was not ungrateful for the silence. He had plenty to keep his mind occupied. He sat smoking, busy with his own thoughts.

The evening was cold and pitch black by the time they had left the outer suburbs behind and the Rolls turned its long nose into a private driveway. There were thick trees on either side; and after a hundred yards, before there was any sign of the house, Sentinel slowed down to take a sharp curve. As though they had materialized out of the fourth dimension two figures jumped on the car's running boards, one on either side. The Saint could see dimly in the reflection of the headlights the bloated figure and bespectacled, bearded face of the man who had swung open the driving door.

"You vill stop der car, please."

"Vell, vell, vell!" said the Saint mildly. "This is certainly great stuff."

His hand was reaching round for his automatic, but by this time his own door had opened, and the car had jerked to a standstill, for both Mr Sentinel's feet had instinctively trodden hard on the pedals. The cold rim of an automatic inserted itself affectionately into the back of Simon Templar's neck.

"Move one finger and you're dead," said Mr Raddon unimaginatively.

"Brother, unless you're very careful you'll drive that thing out through my Adam's apple," Simon complained.

"What the devil does this mean?" spluttered Sentinel angrily; and he suddenly revved up the engine. "Look out, Templar!" he shouted. "I'm going to drive on."

The automatic that was held only a foot from Sentinel's head thudded down, and the film magnate slumped over the wheel.

"Step out, Saint," ordered Raddon.

The Saint stepped. He always knew instinctively when to resist and when not to resist. As his feet trod on hard gravel the gross figure came round the back of the car like some evil monster of the night, and gloved hands went rapidly over the Saint and deprived him of his gun. Then he was told to walk forward. Almost at once he was brought to a halt against the rear of a small delivery van parked in the darkness under a tree with its doors open. A sudden violent shove from behind sent him pitching headlong into it; and the doors slammed behind him with a heavy crash. In another moment the engine roared to life, and the truck lurched forward.

X

Simon had one compensation. The opposition had not waited to search him thoroughly or to bind his wrists and ankles in the approved style. The truck was evidently considered to be secure enough as a temporary prison. Which, in fact, it was. When the Saint heaved against the closed doors he soon came to the conclusion that they were sufficiently strong to hold him in for some time. Wherefore, with his characteristic philosophy, he made himself as comfortable as he could and set out to relieve the tedium of the journey with a cigarette. At least he had gone into the trap with his eyes open, so he had no valid grounds for whining.

He judged that the truck had driven through a hidden path between the trees and had then bumped across a field. After that it had gained a road, and now it was bowling along more smoothly. The journey proved to be comparatively short. Within ten or fifteen minutes there was no longer any sound of other traffic, and the road surface over which the truck was travelling became more rutty and uneven. Then with a giddy swing to the near side the truck left the road again and ran evenly for a few seconds on a level drive before it stopped. For a little while it backed and manoeuvred; and then the sound of the engine died away. There was a slight delay, in which he heard occasional murmurs of voices without being able to detect any recognizable words. It was just possible that a red carpet was being laid down for him, but somehow he doubted it. Then there was a rattle at the doors, and they were flung open. Three powerful electric flashlights blazed on him.

"If I make the slightest resistance I suppose I shall be converted into a colander?" Simon remarked calmly.

"I'm just trying to save you the trouble of giving the customary warnings—"

"Get out," Raddon's voice ordered shortly.

Simon obeyed. He was unable to see much of his surroundings, for the truck had been backed up against a crumbling stone doorway, and the torchlights were so concentrated on him that practically everything else was in black shadow.

Two of the men closed in on him as his feet touched the ground, ramming their guns into his sides. He was thrust on through the doorway into what seemed to be a bare and damp and uninhabited hall and halted with his face to one bleak stone wall. Then while a gun was still held against his spine swift and efficient hands went over him again. His pockets were completely emptied, even to his cigarette case, his automatic lighter and his loose change; and one of the investigating hands felt along his sleeve and removed the knife strapped to his forearm. After the demonstration he had given in Bryerby House, thought the Saint, that was only to be expected; but he would have been happier if it had been overlooked as it had been so many times before.

"So!" came the Z-Man's sneering voice. "The knife, it voss somevere, und it we find. Goot! Mit throwings you are through!"

"You've got beyond the Dennis stage now, brother," said the Saint appreciatively, although he was now without a weapon of any kind. "I can only assume that you must have been reading the Katzenjammer Kids."

A rope was pulled tightly around his wrists, pinioning them together in front of him. Again he was told to move, and he found himself ascending a spiral staircase of vertiginous steepness. Most of the treads were broken and rotting and creaked alarmingly under his weight. The staircase wound itself like a corkscrew around the inner wall of a round tower, which rose straight up from what he had first taken for a sort of hall. At one time, no doubt, there had been a guarding balustrade on the off side; but this had long since ceased to exist, and there was nothing between the climber and a sheer drop to the flagstones below. At the top he stepped off the last tread onto the floor of what might once have been a small turret room, but which was now hardly more than an unrailed ledge suspended over the black abyss. The only windows were two narrow embrasures through which he could see nothing but darkness. He was placed against the wall away from the stairs and close to the edge of the floor, and the other end of the rope around his wrists was run through a heavy iron ring set in the masonry above his head and made fast.

"I can still kick," he observed solicitously. "Are you sure you're not taking a lot of chances?"

"That will not be for long," said the Z-Man.

A block of stone weighing about a hundredweight, with a rope round it, was dragged across the floor, and the rope was tied round the Saint's ankles.

"You vill kick now?" asked the Z-Man. "Yess?"

"I fancy—no," answered the Saint.

He moved his hands experimentally. His wrists were only held by a slipknot. If he could drag a little slack out of the rope where it was tied to the ring he might be able to get them free. He wondered why he had been tied so carelessly; and the next moment he knew. As if in answer to a prearranged signal, Raddon stepped forward and with an effort pushed the rock tied to the Saint's feet off the ledge. It dragged the Saint's legs after it; and the slipknot came tight again instantly as the pull came on it. Simon hung there, excruciatingly stretched out, with only the cord on his wrists to save him from being dragged over the edge.

The Z-Man came closer.

"You know why you are here?" he asked. "You haff interfered with my affairs."

"Considerably," Simon agreed.

In that confined space the light of the torches was reflected from the walls sufficiently to show the men behind them. Besides the Z-Man and Raddon, the third member of the party, as Simon had suspected, was Welmont, of taxicab fame. The two minor Z-Men stood a little behind and to either side of their leader.

The Z-Man put away his torch and took the Saint's own knife out of his pocket.

"You vill tell me how much you know," he said. "Tell me this, my Saint, und your fine looks vill still be yours."

He caressed the knife in his gloved hand and brought it suggestively forward so that the light glinted on the polished blade.

"So we now attempt to make the victim's blood run cold, do we?" said the Saint amusedly, although his joints felt as if they were being torn apart on the rack. "I take it that you're in the mood for one of your celebrated beauty treatments. Why don't you operate on yourself first, laddie? You look as if it would improve you."

"Tell me vot you know!" shouted the Z-Man furiously. "I giff you just one minute."

"And after I've done the necessary spilling I suppose you slit my gizzard with the grapefruit cutter and then bury my remains deeply under the fragrant sod," said the Saint sardonically. "Nothing doing, slug. It's not good enough. I've made myself a hell of a nuisance to you, and you won't be satisfied until I'm as dead as—Mercia Landon."

"You fool," screamed the Z-Man. "I mean vot I say!"

"That makes us even," said the Saint. "But I'm not a film actress, remember. Carving your alphabetical or-

namentations on my face won't decrease my earning ca-
pacity by a cent. I'm surprised at your moderation. Now
that you've got me in your ker-lutches I wonder you
don't flay the skin off my back."

His utter indifference to the peril he was in was
breath-taking. The mockery of his blue eyes and the cool
insolence of his voice had something epic about it, as if
he had turned back the clock to days when men lived
and died with that same ageless carelessness. And yet
even while he spoke his ears were listening. Events had
moved faster than he had anticipated. The Z-Man's lofty
eyrie, too, was a factor of the entertainment that Simon
had not allowed for. Those crumbling stairs couldn't be
climbed easily and quietly. . . . Time was the essential
factor now; and the Saint was beginning to realize that
the support upon which he was relying was not at hand—
while he was not so much at the mercy of a man as of
a homicidal maniac.

The Z-Man was within arm's length of him now.

"No, I do not slit your gizzard," he said huskily. "I
tell you vot I do. I only cut der rope vot hold you up.
Und then der stone pulls you down, und we take off der
ropes, und you haf had an accident und fallen down. Do
you understand?"

The Saint understood very well. He could feel the
dizzy emptiness under his dangling toes. But he still
smiled.

"Well, why don't you get on with it?" he said taunt-
ingly. "Or have you lost your nerve?"

"You crazy fool! You think you are funny! But if I
take you at your word—"

"You're getting careless with that beautiful accent,"
mocked the Saint. "If you say 'vot,' you ought to say
'vord.' The trouble with you is that you're such a lousy
actor. Now if you'd been any good—"

"You asked for it," said the other in a horrible whisper and slashed at the rope from which the Saint hung.

And at the same moment the Saint made his own gamble. The fingers of his right hand strained up, closed on the iron ring from which he was suspended, tightened their grip and held it. The strain on his sinews shot redhot needles through him; and yet he had a sense of serene confidence, a feeling of seraphic inevitability, that no pain could suppress. He had goaded the Z-Man, as he had anticipated; and he had been waiting with every nerve and muscle for the one solitary chance that the fall of the cards offered—a game fighting chance to win through. And the chance had come off.

The rope no longer held him from plunging down to almost certain death, but the steel strength of his own fingers did. And as the rope parted the slipknot had loosened so that he could wrench his left hand free.

"Thanks a lot, sweetheart," said the Saint.

A hawk would have had difficulty in following the movements that came immediately afterwards. As the Z-Man gasped with sudden fear a circle of wrought steel whipped across his shoulder, swung him completely round and placed him so that his back was towards the Saint. Then the Saint's left hand snaked under his opponent's left arm, flashed up to his neck and secured a half nelson that was as solid as if it had been carved out of stone.

"We can now indulge in skylarking and song," said the Saint. "I'll do the skylarking, and you can provide the song."

To some extent he was right; but the Z-Man's song was not so much musical as reminiscent of the shriek of a lost locomotive. Some men might have got out of that half nelson, particularly as the Saint was still crucified between his precarious grip on the ring and the weight that was trying to drag him down into the black void;

but the Z-Man knew nothing about wrestling, and all the strength seemed to have gone out of him. Moreover, the Saint's thumb on one side of his captive's neck and his lean brown fingers on the other were crushing with deadly effect into his victim's carotid arteries. Scientifically applied, this treatment can produce unconsciousness in a few seconds; but Simon was at a disadvantage, for half his strength was devoted to fighting the relentless drag on his ankles.

Raddon and Welmont started forward too late. The Saint's wintry laugh met them at their first step.

"If anything happens," he said with pitiless clarity, "your pal goes over first."

They checked as if they had run into an invisible wall; and Raddon's Gumpish face showed white as his torch jumped in his hand.

"For God's sake," he gasped hoarsely. "Wait—"

"Is dat you, boss?" bawled a foghorn voice far below; and the Saint's smile became a shade more blissful in spite of the wrenching agony in his right shoulder.

"This is me, Hoppy," he said. "You'd better come up quickly—and look out for someone coming down." He looked over the shuddering bundle of the Z-Man at Raddon and Welmont, still frozen in their tracks.

"There's no way out for you unless you can fly," he said. "How would you like to be a pair of angels?"

They made no attempt to graduate into a pair of angels. They stood very still as Hoppy Uniatz crashed off the stairs onto the ledge, followed by Patricia, and briskly removed their guns. A moment later an arm like a tree trunk took the weight off the Saint's hand and hauled him back to the safety of the floor.

Patricia was touching the Saint as if to make sure that he was real.

"Are you all right, boy?" she was asking tremulously.

"I was afraid we'd be too late. They'd locked the outside door, and Hoppy was afraid of making a noise—"

The Saint kissed her.

"You were in plenty of time," he said and yanked the Z-Man clear of the edge of the floor. "Think you could hold him, Hoppy?"

"Wit' one finger," said Mr Uniatz scornfully.

With one swift hop that was in itself a complete justification of his nickname he heaved the Z-Man to his feet from behind and held him in a gorilla grip. The Z-Man's struggles were as futile as the wrigglings of a fly between the fingers of a small boy. And the Saint retrieved his knife and tested the point on his thumb.

"Hold him just like that, Hoppy," he said grimly, "so that his tummy occupies the centre of the stage. I want to do some surgery of my own."

With a swift movement that made Patricia catch her breath and shut her eyes quickly he thrust the knife deeply and forcefully into the Z-Man's protruding stomach. There was a loud squealing hiss, and the patient deflated like a punctured tire.

"I just wanted to see whether it would make a squashy noise or merely explode," said the Saint placidly. "You can open your eyes, darling. There's no mess on the floor. Mr Vell is mostly composed of air."

With a swift movement he yanked off his victim's hat, wig, glasses and beard.

"Miss Sheila Ireland, I believe," murmured the Saint courteously.

XI

Patricia found her voice first.

"But I thought you told me Sentinel was the Z-Man," she said weakly. "We left Orace to tie him up—"

"I didn't say so," answered the Saint. "I told you that I'd met Comrade Sentinel, and I thought I knew who the Z-Man was. But I wanted you to tell the girls about Comrade Sentinel because I knew she'd remember that he knew about her affair with Raddon, and I knew she'd be scared that he might say something that'd start me thinking, and I knew she'd get the wind up and feel that she had to do something about it—that is, if my suspicions were right. And I was damn right!"

"I wondered why she suddenly decided that she couldn't stay away from the studio a little while after I told her the news," Patricia said slowly. "But I never thought . . ."

"I did," said the Saint. "I did most of my thinking in Sentinel's office. He was twiddling a pencil—and all at once I remembered that when I was in Bryerby House the Z-Man had been twiddling a pencil too. Only the Z-Man had a different twiddle. Everybody has his own distinctive nervous habits. I started thinking about the Z-Man's twiddle, wondering where else I'd seen it; and all at once it dawned on me that it was exactly like the way Sheila Ireland had been twiddling her cigarette holder last night when she was telling us her tale of woe. It nearly knocked me over backwards."

He looked across at the dishevelled girl who was still writhing hysterically in Hoppy's relentless grasp, with the smeared remains of her make-up disfiguring her face; and his eyes were hard and merciless.

"It wasn't a bad idea to make yourself up not only like a man, but like a fat, repulsive Zeidelmann," he said. "You nearly fooled me until I saw you running away from Bryerby House. There's something funny about the way a woman runs, and that started me thinking. Even then I didn't get the idea, but I was ready for it. You did the voice pretty well too; but that was your business.

You only fell down on the little details like pencil-twiddling. And of course nobody would expect you to be a woman. But you were woman enough to make Andy Gump go on putting his head in the noose to try and please you even after he'd come out of stir for the cheques he forged to buy you jewelry. And you were woman enough to know what the threat of disfigurement would mean to a woman." The Saint's voice was like icy water flowing down a glacier. "You got it both ways. You put the boodle into your own bank account, and at the same time your rivals were having breakdowns and getting thrown out of the running and letting you climb higher. . . . I wonder how you'd like it if we made the punishment fit the crime?"

The girl strained madly against Hoppy's iron hands.

"Let me go!" she screamed. "You swine! You couldn't—"

"Let her go, Hoppy," said the Saint quietly.

Mr Uniatz unlocked his fingers, and the girl tore herself free and stood swaying on the edge of the floor.

"Would Andy still love you if you had a Z carved on your face?" asked the Saint speculatively.

He moved the knife in his hand in an unmistakable gesture.

He had no intention of using it, but he wanted her to feel some of the mental agony that she had given to others before he dealt with her in the only way he could. But all the things he would have liked to do were in his voice, and the girl was too demented with terror to distinguish between fine shades of meaning. She gaped at him in stupefied horror as he took a step towards her; and then, with an inarticulate, despairing shriek, she flung herself backwards into the black pit below. . . .

Raddon started forward with a queer animal moan,

but Hoppy's gun whipped up and thrust him back. And the Saint looked at him.

"It's no use, Andy," he said with his first tinge of pity. "You backed the wrong horse."

He slid his knife back into its sheath and put an arm around Patricia.

"Where are we?" he asked in a matter-of-fact voice.

"This is some sort of old ruin with a modern house built into one wing of it." She spoke mechanically, with her eyes still hypnotized by the dark silence into which Sheila Ireland had disappeared. "I suppose it belonged to her. . . ."

The Saint buttoned his coat. Life went on, and business was still business.

"Then it probably contains a safe with some boodle in it," he said. "I know a few good causes that could use it. And then we'd better hustle back and untie Comrade Sentinel before he bursts a blood vessel. We'll have to take him back to Weybridge and add him to Beatrice and Irene for the alibi we're going to need when Claud Eustace hears about this. Let's keep moving."

THE ORACLE OF THE DOG
by G. K. Chesterton

G. K. Chesterton (1874–1936) was one of England's eminent men of letters—novelist, short story writer, playwright, poet, essayist, editor, and even illustrator of his own works and those of his close friends Hilaire Belloc and E. C. Bentley. Although he published more than 150 books, he is best remembered today for the five volumes of Father Brown short stories beginning with The Innocence of Father Brown *(1911), arguably the best volume of short detective stories ever written.*

"The Oracle of the Dog," more of a novelette in length than a true novella, is considered by many to be the very best of the Father Brown stories, and was chosen as one of the best mysteries of all time in a 1983 vote by members of the Mystery Writers of America. It blends religion and paradox and an impossible crime in a manner that remains uniquely Chestertonian. Following its first magazine publication in 1923, "The Oracle of the Dog" was collected in The Incredulity of Father Brown *(1926).*

Though he was a writer on Catholic subjects for much of his life, Chesterton was not actually converted to Roman Catholicism until 1922. From 1928 until his death, G. K. Chesterton served as the first president of the Detection Club.

"Yes," said Father Brown, "I always like a dog, so long as he isn't spelt backwards."

Those who are quick in talking are not always quick in listening. Sometimes even their brilliancy produces a sort of stupidity. Father Brown's friend and companion was a young man with a stream of ideas and stories, an enthusiastic young man named Fiennes, with eager blue eyes and blond hair that seemed to be brushed back, not merely with a hair-brush but with the wind of the world as he rushed through it. But he stopped in the torrent of his talk in a momentary bewilderment before he saw the priest's very simple meaning.

"You mean that people make too much of them?" he said. "Well, I don't know. They're marvellous creatures. Sometimes I think they know a lot more than we do."

Father Brown said nothing, but continued to stroke the head of the big retriever in a half-abstracted but apparently soothing fashion.

"Why," said Fiennes, warming again to his monologue, "there was a dog in the case I've come to see you about: what they call the 'Invisible Murder Case,' you know. It's a strange story, but from my point of view the dog is about the strangest thing in it. Of course, there's the mystery of the crime itself, and how old Druce can have been killed by somebody else when he was all alone in the summer-house—"

The hand stroking the dog stopped for a moment in its rhythmic movement, and Father Brown said calmly: "Oh, it was a summer-house, was it?"

"I thought you'd read all about it in the papers," answered Fiennes, "Stop a minute; I believe I've got a cutting that will give you all the particulars." He produced a strip of newspaper from his pocket and handed it to the priest, who began to read it, holding it close to his blinking eyes with one hand while the other continued its half-conscious caresses of the dog. It looked like the parable of a man not letting his right hand know what his left hand did.

"Many mystery stories, about men murdered behind locked doors and windows, and murderers escaping without means of entrance and exit, have come true in the course of the extraordinary events at Cranston on the coast of Yorkshire, where Colonel Druce was found stabbed from behind by a dagger that has entirely disappeared from the scene, and apparently even from the neighbourhood.

"The summer-house in which he died was indeed accessible at one entrance, the ordinary doorway which looked down the central walk of the garden towards the house. But, by a combination of events almost to be called a coincidence, it appears that both the path and the entrance were watched during the crucial time, and there is a chain of witnesses who confirm each other. The summer-house stands at the extreme end of the garden, where there is no exit or entrance of any kind. The central garden path is a lane between two ranks of tall delphiniums, planted so close that any stray step off the path would leave its traces; and both path and plants run right up to the very mouth of the summer-house, so that no straying from that straight path could fail to be observed, and no other mode of entrance can be imagined.

"Patrick Floyd, secretary of the murdered man, testified that he had been in a position to overlook the whole garden from the time when Colonel Druce last appeared alive in the doorway to the time when he was found dead; as he, Floyd, had been on the top of a step-ladder clipping the garden hedge. Janet Druce, the dead man's daughter, confirmed this, saying that she had sat on the terrace of the house throughout that time and had seen Floyd at his work. Touching some part of the time, this is again supported by Donald Druce, her brother— who overlooked the garden—standing at his bedroom window in his dressing-gown, for he had risen late. Lastly, the account is consistent with that given by Dr Valentine, a neighbour, who called for a time to talk with Miss Druce on the terrace, and by the Colonel's solicitor, Mr Aubrey Traill, who was apparently the last to see the murdered man alive—presumably with the exception of the murderer.

"All are agreed that the course of events was as follows: About half-past three in the afternoon, Miss Druce went down the path to ask her father when he would like tea; but he said he did not want any and was waiting to see Traill, his lawyer, who was to be sent to him in the summer-house. The girl then came away and met Traill coming down the path; she directed him to her father and he went in as directed. About half an hour afterwards he came out again, the Colonel coming with him to the door and showing himself to all appearance in health and even high spirits. He had been somewhat annoyed earlier in the day by his sons's irregular hours, but seemed to recover his temper in a perfectly normal fasion, and had been rather markedly genial in receiving other visitors, including two of his nephews, who came over for the day. But as these were out walking during the whole period of the tragedy, they had no evidence to give. It is said, indeed, that the Colonel was not on very good terms with Dr Valentine, but that gentleman only had a brief interview with the daughter of the house, to whom he is supposed to be paying serious attentions.

"Traill, the solicitor, says he left the Colonel entirely alone in the summer-house, and this is confirmed by Floyd's bird's-eye view of the garden, which showed nobody else passing the only entrance. Ten minutes later, Miss Druce again went down the garden and had not reached the end of the path when she saw her father, who was conspicuous by his white linen coat, lying in a heap on the floor. She uttered a scream which brought others to the spot, and on entering the place they found the Colonel lying dead beside his basket-chair, which was also up-set. Dr Valentine, who was still in the immediate neighbour-hood, testified that the wound was made by some sort of stiletto, entering under the shoulder-blade and piercing the heart. The police have searched the neighbourhood for such a weapon, but no trace of it can be found."

"So Colonel Druce wore a white coat, did he?" said Father Brown as he put down the paper.

"Trick he learnt in the tropics," replied Fiennes, with some wonder. "He'd had some queer adventures there, by his own account; and I fancy his dislike of Valentine was connected with the doctor coming from the tropics, too. But it's all an infernal puzzle. The account there is pretty accurate; I didn't see the tragedy, in the sense of the discovery; I was out walking with the young nephews and the dog—the dog I wanted to tell you about. But

I saw the stage set for it as described; the straight lane between the blue flowers right up to the dark entrance, and the lawyer going down it in his blacks and his silk hat, and the red head of the secretary showing high above the green hedge as he worked on it with his shears. Nobody could have mistaken that red head at any distance; and if people say they saw it there all the time, you may be sure they did. This red-haired secretary, Floyd, is quite a character; a breathless bounding sort of fellow, always doing everybody's work as he was doing the gardener's. I think he is an American; he's certainly got the American view of life—what they call the view-point, bless 'em."

"What about the lawyer?" asked Father Brown.

There was a silence and then Fiennes spoke quite slowly for him. "Traill struck me as a singular man. In his fine black clothes he was almost foppish, yet you can hardly call him fashionable. For he wore a pair of long, luxuriant black whiskers such as haven't been seen since Victorian times. He had rather a fine grave face and a fine grave manner, but every now and then he seemed to remember to smile. And when he showed his white teeth he seemed to lose a little of his dignity, and there was something faintly fawning about him. It may have been only embarrassment, for he would also fidget with his cravat and his tie-pin, which were at once handsome and unusual, like himself. If I could think of anybody—but what's the good, when the whole thing's impossible? Nobody knows who did it. Nobody knows how it could be done. At least there's only one exception I'd make, and that's why I really mentioned the whole thing. The dog knows."

Father Brown sighed and then said absently: "You were there as a friend of young Donald, weren't you? He didn't go on your walk with you?"

"No," replied Fiennes smiling. "The young scoundrel had gone to bed that morning and got up that afternoon. I went with his cousins, two young officers from India, and our conversation was trivial enough. I remember the elder, whose name I think is Herbert Druce and who is an authority on horse-breeding, talked about nothing but a mare he had bought and the moral character of the man who sold her; while his brother Harry seemed to be brooding on his bad luck at Monte Carlo. I only mention it to show you, in the light of what happened on our walk, that there was nothing psychic about us. The dog was the only mystic in our company."

"What sort of a dog was he?" asked the priest.

"Same breed as that one," answered Fiennes. "That's what started me off on the story, your saying you didn't believe in believing in a dog. He's a big black retriever, named Nox, and a suggestive name, too; for I think what he did a darker mystery than the murder. You know Druce's house and garden are by the sea; we walked about a mile from it along the sands and then turned back, going the other way. We passed a rather curious rock called the Rock of Fortune, famous in the neighbourhood because it's one of those examples of one stone barely balanced on another, so that a touch would knock it over. It is not really very high but the hanging outline of it makes it look a little wild and sinister; at least it made it look so to me, for I don't imagine my jolly young companions were afflicted with the picturesque. But it may be that I was beginning to feel an atmosphere; for just then the question arose of whether it was time to go back to tea, and even then I think I had a premonition that time counted for a good deal in the business. Neither Herbert Druce nor I had a watch, so we called out to his brother, who was some paces behind, having stopped to light his pipe under the hedge. Hence it happened that he shouted out the hour, which was twenty past four, in his big voice through the growing twilight; and somehow the loudness of it made it sound like the proclamation of something tremendous. His unconsciousness seemed to make it all the more so; but that was always the way with omens; and particular ticks of the clock were really very ominous things that afternoon. According to Dr Valentine's testimony, poor Druce had actually died just about half-past four.

"Well, they said we needn't go home for ten minutes, and we walked a little farther along the sands, doing nothing in particular—throwing stones for the dog and throwing sticks into the sea for him to swim after. But to me the twilight seemed to grow oddly oppressive, and the very shadow of the top-heavy Rock of Fortune lay on me like a load. And then the curious thing happened. Nox had just brought back Herbert's walking-stick out of the sea and his brother had thrown his in also. The dog swam out again, but just about what must have been the stroke of the half-hour, he stopped swimming. He came back again on the shore and stood in front of us. Then he suddenly threw up his head and sent up a howl or wail of woe—if ever I heard one in the world.

" 'What the devil's the matter with the dog?' asked Herbert; but none of us could answer. There ws a long silence after the brute's wailing and whining died away on the desolate shore; and then the silence was broken. As I live, it was broken by a faint and far-off shriek, like the shriek of a woman from beyond the hedges inland. We didn't know what it was then; but we knew afterwards. It was the cry the girl gave when she first saw the body of her father."

"You went back, I suppose," said Father Brown patiently. "What happened then?"

"I'll tell you what happened then," said Fiennes with

a grim emphasis. "When we got back into that garden the first thing we saw was Traill, the lawyer; I can see him now with his black hat and black whiskers relieved against the perspective of the blue flowers stretching down to the summer-house, with the sunset and the strange outline of the Rock of Fortune in the distance. His face and figure were in shadow against the sunset; but I swear the white teeth were showing in his head and he was smiling.

"The moment Nox saw that man the dog dashed forward and stood in the middle of the path barking at him madly, murderously, volleying out curses that were almost verbal in their dreadful distinctness of hatred. And the man doubled up and fled along the path between the flowers."

Father Brown sprang to his feet with a startling impatience.

"So the dog denounced him, did he?" he cried. "The oracle of the dog condemned him. Did you see what birds were flying, and are you sure whether they were on the right hand or the left? Did you consult the augurs about the sacrifices? Surely you didn't omit to cut open the dog and examine his entrails. That is the sort of scientific test you heathen humanitarians seem to trust when you are thinking of taking away the life and honour of a man."

Fiennes sat gaping for an instant before he found breath to say: "Why, what's the matter with you? What have I done now?"

A sort of anxiety came back into the priest's eyes—the anxiety of a man who has run against a post in the dark and wonders for a moment whether he has hurt it.

"I'm most awfully sorry," he said with sincere distress. "I beg your pardon for being so rude; pray forgive me."

Fiennes looked at him curiously. "I sometimes think you are more of a mystery than any of the mysteries," he said. "But anyhow, if you don't believe in the mystery of the dog, at least you can't get over the mystery of the man. You can't deny that at the very moment when the beast came back from the sea and bellowed, his master's soul was driven out of his body by the blow of some unseen power that no mortal man can trace or even imagine. And as for the lawyer—I don't go only by the dog—there are other curious details, too. He struck me as a smooth, smiling, equivocal sort of person; and one of his tricks seemed like a sort of hint. You know the doctor and the police were on the spot very quickly; Valentine was brought back when walking away from the house, and he telephoned instantly. That, with the secluded house, small numbers, and enclosed space, made it pretty possible to search everybody who could have been near; and everybody was thoroughly searched—for a weapon. The whole house, garden, and shore were combed for a weapon. The disappearance of the dagger is almost as crazy as the disappearance of man."

"The disappearance of the dagger," said Father Brown, nodding. He seemed to have become suddenly attentive.

"Well," continued Fiennes, "I told you that man Traill had a trick of fidgeting with his tie and tie-pin—especially his tie-pin. His pin, like himself, was at once showy and old-fashioned. It had one of those stones with concentric coloured rings that look like an eye; and his own concentration on it got on my nerves, as if he had been a Cyclops with one eye in the middle of his body. But the pin was not only large but long; and it occurred to me that his anxiety about its adjustment was because it was even longer than it looked; as long as a stiletto in fact."

Father Brown nodded thoughtfully. "Was any other instrument ever suggested?" he asked.

"There was another suggestion," answered Fiennes, "from one of the young Druces—the cousins, I mean. Neither Herbert nor Harry Druce would have struck one at first as likely to be of assistance in scientific detection; but while Herbert was really the traditional type of heavy Dragoon, caring for nothing but horses and being an ornament to the Horse Guards, his younger brother Harry had been in the Indian Police and knew something about such things. Indeed, in his own way he was quite clever; and I rather fancy he had been too clever; I mean he had left the police through breaking some red-tape regulations and taking some sort of risk and responsibility of his own. Anyhow, he was in some sense a detective out of work, and threw himself into this business with more than the ardour of an amateur. And it was with him that I had an argument about the weapon—an argument that led to something new. It began by his countering my description of the dog barking at Traill; and he said that a dog at his worst didn't bark, but growled."

"He was quite right there," observed the priest.

"This young fellow went on to say that, if it came to that, he'd heard Nox growling at other people before then; and among others at Floyd, the secretary. I retorted that his own argument answered itself; for the crime couldn't be brought home to two or three people, and least of all to Floyd, who was as innocent as a harum-scarum schoolboy, and had been seen by everybody all the time perched above the garden hedge with his fan of red hair as conspicuous as a scarlet cockatoo. 'I know there's difficulties anyhow,' said my colleague; 'but I wish you'd come with me down the garden a minute. I want to show you something I don't think any one else has seen.' This was on the very day of the discovery, and the garden was just as it had been. The step-ladder was still standing by the hedge, and just under the hedge my guide stopped and disentangled something from the deep grass. It was the shears used for clipping the hedge, and on the point of one of them was a smear of blood."

There was a short silence, and then Father Brown said suddenly, "What was the lawyer there for?"

"He told us the Colonel sent for him to alter his will," answered Fiennes. "And, by the way, there was another thing about the business of the will that I ought to mention. You see, the will wasn't actually signed in the summer-house that afternoon."

"I suppose not," said Father Brown; "there would have to be two witnesses."

"The lawyer actually came down the day before and it was signed then; but he was sent for again next day because the old man had a doubt about one of the witnesses and had to be reassured."

"Who were the witnesses?" asked Father Brown.

"That's just the point," replied his informant eagerly, "the witnesses were Floyd, the secretary, and this Dr Valentine, the foreign sort of surgeon or whatever he is; and the two have a quarrel. Now I'm bound to say that the secretary is something of a busybody. He's one of those hot and headlong people whose warmth of temperament has unfortunately turned mostly to pugnacity and bristling suspicion; to distrusting people instead of to trusting them. That sort of red-haired red-hot fellow is always either universally credulous or universally incredulous; and sometimes both. He was not only a Jack-of-all-trades, but he knew better than all tradesmen. He not only knew everything, but he warned everybody against everybody. All that must be taken into account in his suspicions about Valentine; but in that particular case there seems to have been something behind it. He said the name of Valentine was not really Valentine. He said he had seen him elsewhere known by the name of Dr Villon. He said it would invalidate the will; of course he was kind enough to explain to the lawyer what the law was on that point. They were both in a frightful wax."

Father Brown laughed. "People often are when they are to witness a will," he said; "for one thing, it means that they can't have any legacy under it. But what did Dr Valentine say? No doubt the universal secretary knew more about the doctor's name than the doctor did. But even the doctor might have some information about his own name."

Fiennes paused a moment before he replied.

"Dr Valentine took it in a curious way. Dr Valentine is a curious man. His appearance is rather striking but very foreign. He is young but wears a beard cut square; and his face is very pale, dreadfully pale and dreadfully serious. His eyes have a sort of ache in them, as if he ought to wear glasses, or had given himself a headache with thinking; but he is quite handsome and always very formally dressed, with a top hat and a dark coat and a little red rosette. His manner is rather cold and haughty, and he has a way of staring at you which is very disconcerting. When thus charged with having changed his name, he merely stared like a sphinx and then said with a little laugh that he supposed Americans had no names to change. At that I think the Colonel also got into a fuss and said all sorts of angry things to the doctor; all the more angry because of the doctor's pretensions to a future place in his family. But I shouldn't have thought much of that but for a few words that I happened to hear later, early in the afternoon of the tragedy. I don't want to make a lot of them, for they weren't the sort of words on which one would like, in the ordinary way, to play the eavesdropper. As I was passing out towards the front gate with my two companions and the dog, I heard voices which told me that Dr Valentine and Miss Druce had withdrawn for a moment into the shadow of the house, in an angle behind a row of flowering plants, and were talking to each other in passionate whisperings—sometimes almost like hissings; for it was something of a lovers' quarrel as well as a lovers' tryst. Nobody repeats the sort of things they said for the most part; but in an unfortunate business like this I'm bound to say that there was repeated more than once a phrase about killing somebody. In fact, the girl seemed to be begging him not to kill somebody, or saying that no provocation could justify killing anybody; which seems an unusual sort of talk to address to a gentleman who has dropped in to tea."

"Do you know," asked the priest, "whether Dr Valentine seemed to be very angry after the scene with the secretary and the Colonel—I mean about witnessing the will?"

"By all accounts," replied the other, "he wasn't half so angry as the secretary was. It was the secretary who went away raging after witnessing the will."

"And now," said Father Brown, "what about the will itself?"

"The Colonel was a very wealthy man, and his will was important. Traill wouldn't tell us the alteration at that stage, but I have since heard only this morning in fact—that most of the money was transferred from the son to the daughter. I told you that Druce was wild with my friend Donald over his dissipated hours."

"The question of motive has been rather over-shadowed by the question of method," observed Father Brown thoughtfully. "At that moment, apparently, Miss Druce was the immediate gainer by the death."

"Good God! What a cold-blooded way of talking," cried Fiennes, staring at him. "You don't really mean to hint that she—"

"Is she going to marry that Dr Valentine?" asked the other.

"Some people are against it," answered his friend. "But he is liked and respected in the place and is a skilled and devoted surgeon."

"So devoted a surgeon," said Father Brown, "that he had surgical instruments with him when he went to call on the young lady at tea-time. For he must have used a lancet or something, and he never seems to have gone home."

Fiennes sprang to his feet and looked at him in a heat of inquiry. "You suggest he might have used the very same lancet—"

Father Brown shook his head. "All these suggestions are fancies just now," he said. "The problem is not who did it or what did it, but how it was done. We might find many men and even many tools—pins and shears and lancets. But how did a man get into the room? How did even a pin get into it?"

He was staring reflectively at the ceiling as he spoke, but as he said the last words his eye cocked in an alert fashion as if he had suddenly seen a curious fly on the ceiling.

"Well, what would you do about it?" asked the young man. "You have a lot of experience; what would you advise now?"

"I'm afraid I'm not much use," said Father Brown with a sigh. "I can't suggest very much without having ever been near the place or the people. For the moment you can only go on with local inquiries. I gather that your friend from the Indian Police is more or less in charge of your inquiry down there. I should run down and see how he is getting on. See what he's been doing in the way of amateur detection. There may be news already."

As his guests, the biped and the quadruped, disappeard, Father Brown took up his pen and went back to his interrupted occupation of planning a course of lectures on the Encyclical *Rerum Novarum*. The subject was a large one and he had to re-cast it more than once, so that he was somewhat similarly employed some two days later when the big black dog again came bounding into the room and sprawled all over him with enthusiasm and excitement. The master who followed the dog shared the excitement if not the enthusiasm. He had been excited in a less pleasant fashion, for his blue eyes seemed to start from his head and his eager face was even a little pale.

"You told me," he said abruptly and without preface, "to find out what Harry Druce was doing. Do you know what he's done?"

The priest did not reply, and the young man went on in jerky tones:

"I'll tell you what he's done. He's killed himself."

Father Brown's lips moved only faintly, and there was nothing practical about what he was saying—nothing that has anything to do with this story or this world.

"You give me the creeps sometimes," said Fiennes. "Did you—did you expect this?"

"I thought it possible," said Father Brown; "that was why I asked you to go and see what he was doing. I hoped you might not be too late."

"It was I who found him," said Fiennes rather huskily. "It was the ugliest and most uncanny thing I ever knew. I went down that old garden again, and I knew there was something new and unnatural about it besides the murder. The flowers still tossed about in blue masses on each side of the black entrance into the old grey summer-house; but to me the blue flowers looked like blue devils dancing before some dark cavern of the underworld. I looked all round, everything seemed to be in its ordinary place. But the queer notion grew on me that there was something wrong with the very shape of the sky. And then I saw what it was. The Rock of Fortune always rose in the background beyond the garden hedge and against the sea. And the Rock of Fortune was gone."

Father Brown had lifted his head and was listening intently.

"It was as if a mountain had walked away out of a landscape or a moon fallen from the sky; though I knew, of course, that a touch at any time would have tipped the thing over. Something possessed me and I rushed down that garden path like the wind and went crashing through that hedge as if it were a spider's web. It was a thin hedge really, though its undisturbed trimness had made it serve all the purposes of a wall. On the shore I found the loose rock fallen from its pedestal; and poor Harry Druce lay like a wreck underneath it. One arm was thrown round it in a sort of embrace as if he had pulled it down on himself; and on the broad brown sands beside it, in large crazy lettering, he had scrawled the words: 'The Rock of Fortune falls on the Fool.'"

"It was the Colonel's will that did that," observed Father Brown. "The young man had staked everything on profiting himself by Donald's disgrace, especially when his uncle sent for him on the same day as the lawyer, and welcomed him with so much warmth. Otherwise he was done; he'd lost his police job; he was beggared at Monte Carlo. And he killed himself when he found he'd killed his kinsman for nothing."

"Here, stop a minute!" cried the staring Fiennes. "You're going too fast for me."

"Talking about the will, by the way," continued Father Brown calmly "before I forget it, or we go on to bigger things, there was a simple explanation, I think, of all that business about the doctor's name. I rather fancy I have heard both names before somewhere. The doctor is really a French nobleman with the title of the Marquis de Villon. But he is also an ardent Republican and has abandoned his title and fallen back on the forgotten family surname. "With your Citizen Riquetti you have puzzled Europe for ten days."

"What is that?" asked the young man blankly.

"Never mind," said the priest. "Nine times out of ten it is a rascally thing to change one's name; but this was a piece of fine fanaticism. That's the point of his sarcasm about Americans having no names—that is, no titles. Now in England the Marquis of Hartington is never called Mr Hartington; but in France the Marquis de Villon is called M de Villon. So it might well look like a change of name. As for the talk about killing, I fancy that also was a point of French etiquette. The doctor was talking about challenging Floyd to a duel, and the girl was trying to dissuade him."

"Oh, I *see*," cried Fiennes slowly. "Now I understand what she meant."

"And what is that about?" asked his companion, smiling.

"Well," said the young man, "it was something that happened to me just before I found that poor fellow's body; only the catastrophe drove it out of my head. I suppose it's hard to remember a little romantic idyll when you've just come on top of a tragedy. But as I went down the lanes leading to the Colonel's old place I met his daughter walking with Dr Valentine. She was in mourning, of course, and he always wore black as if he were going to a funeral; but I can't say that their faces were very funereal. Never have I seen two people looking in their own way more respectably radiant and cheerful. They stopped and saluted me, and then she told me they were married and living in a little house on the outskirts of the town, where the doctor was continuing his practice. This rather surprised me, because I knew that her old father's will had left her his property; and I hinted at it delicately by saying I was going along to her father's old place and had half expected to meet her there. But she only laughed and said: 'Oh, we've given up all that. My husband doesn't like heiresses.' And I discovered with some astonishment they really had insisted on restoring the property to poor Donald; so I hope he's had a healthy shock and will treat it sensibly. There was never much really the matter with him: he was very young and his father was not very wise. But it was in connexion with that that she said something I didn't understand at the time; but now I'm sure it must be as you say. She said with a sort of sudden and splendid arrogance that was entirely altruistic:

" 'I hope it'll stop that red-haired fool from fussing any more about the will. Does he think my husband, who has given up a crest and a coronet as old as the Crusades for his principles, would kill an old man in a summer-house for a legacy like that?' Then she laughed again and said, 'My husband isn't killing anybody except in the way of business. Why, he didn't even ask his friends to call on the secretary.' Now, of course, I see what she meant."

"I see part of what she meant, of course," said Father Brown. "What did she mean exactly by the secretary fussing about the will?"

Fiennes smiled as he answered. "I wish you knew the secretary, Father Brown. It would be a joy to you to watch him make things hum, as he calls it. He made the house of mourning hum. He filled the funeral with all the snap and zip of the brightest sporting event. There was no holding him, after something had really happened. I've told you how he used to oversee the gardener as he did the garden, and how he instructed the lawyer in the law. Needless to say, he also instructed the surgeon in the practice of surgery; and as the surgeon was Dr Valentine, you may be sure it ended in accusing him of something worse than bad surgery. The secretary got it fixed in his red head that the doctor had committed the crime, and when the police arrived he was perfectly sublime. Need I say that he became, on the spot, the greatest of all amateur detectives? Sherlock Holmes never towered over Scotland Yard with more Titanic intellectual pride and scorn than Colonel Druce's private secretary over the police investigating Colonel Druce's death. I tell you it was a joy to see him. He strode about with an abstracted air, tossing his scarlet crest of hair and giving curt impatient replies. Of course it was his demeanour during these days that made Druce's daughter so wild with him. Of course he had a theory. It's just the sort of theory a man would have in a book; and Floyd is the sort of man who ought to be in a book. He'd be better fun and less bother in a book."

"What was his theory?" asked the other.

"Oh, it was full of pep," replied Fiennes gloomily. "It would have been glorious copy if it could have held together for ten minutes longer. He said the Colonel was still alive when they found him in the summer-house, and the doctor killed him with the surgical instrument on pretence of cutting the clothes."

"I see," said the priest. "I suppose he was lying flat on his face on the mud floor as a form of siesta."

"It's wonderful what hustle will do," continued his informant. "I believe Floyd would have got his great theory into the papers at any rate, and perhaps had the doctor arrested, when all these things were blown sky high as if by dynamite by the discovery of that dead body lying under the Rock of Fortune. And that's what we come back to after all. I suppose the suicide is almost a confession. But nobody will ever know the whole story."

There was a silence, and then the priest said modestly: "I rather think I know the whole story."

Fiennes stared, "But look here," he cried; "how do you come to know the whole story, or to be sure it's the true story? You've been sitting here a hundred miles away writing a sermon; do you mean to tell me you really know what happened already? If you've really come to the end, where in the world do you begin? What started you off with your own story?"

Father Brown jumped up with a very unusual excitement and his first exclamation was like an explosion.

"The dog!" he cried. "The dog, of course! You had the whole story in your hands in the business of the dog on the beach, if you'd only noticed the dog properly."

Fiennes stared still more. "But you told me before that my feelings about the dog were all nonsense, and the dog had nothing to do with it."

"The dog had everything to do with it," said Father Brown, "as you'd have found out if you'd only treated the dog as a dog, and not as God Almighty judging the souls of men."

He paused in an embarrassed way for a moment, and then said, with a rather pathetic air of apology: "The truth is, I happen to be awfully fond of dogs. And it seemed to me that in all this lurid halo of dog superstitions nobody was really thinking about the poor dog at all. To begin with a small point, about his barking at the lawyer or growling at the secretary. You asked how I could guess things a hundred miles away; but honestly it's mostly to your credit, for you described people so well that I know the types. A man like Traill, who frowns usually and smiles suddenly, a man who fiddles with things, especially at his throat, is a nervous, easily embarrassed man. I shouldn't wonder if Floyd, the efficient secretary, is nervy and jumpy, too; those Yankee hustlers often are. Otherwise he wouldn't have cut his fingers on the shears and dropped them when he heard Janet Druce scream.

"Now dogs hate nervous people. I don't know whether they make the dog nervous, too; or whether, being after all a brute, he is a bit of a bully; or whether his canine vanity (which is colossal) is simply offended at not being liked. But anyhow there was nothing in poor Nox protesting against those people, except that he disliked them for being afraid of him. Now I know you're awfully clever, and nobody of sense sneers at cleverness. But I sometimes fancy, for instance, that you are too clever to understand animals. Sometimes you are too clever to understand men, especially when they act almost as simply as animals. Animals are very literal; they live in a world of truisms. Take this case: a dog barks at a man and a man runs away from a dog. Now you do not seem to be quite simple enough to see the fact: that the dog barked because he disliked the man and the man fled because he was frightened of the dog. They had no other motives and they needed none; but you must read psychological mysteries into it and suppose the dog had super-normal vision, and was a mysterious mouthpiece of doom. You must suppose the man was running away, not from the dog but from the hangman. And yet, if you come to think of it, all this deeper psychology is exceedingly improbable. If the dog really could completely and consciously realize the murderer of his master he wouldn't stand yapping as he might at a curate at a tea-party; he's much more likely to fly at his throat. And on the other hand, do you really think a man who had hardened his heart to murder an old friend and then walk about smiling at the old friend's family, under the eyes of his old friend's daughter and post-mortem doctor—do you think a man like that would be doubled up by mere remorse because a dog barked? He might feel the tragic irony of it; it might shake his soul, like any other tragic trifle. But he wouldn't rush madly the length of a garden to escape from the only witness whom he knew to be unable to talk. People have a panic like that when they are frightened, not of tragic ironies, but of teeth. The whole thing is simpler than you can understand.

"But when we come to that business by the seashore, things are much more interesting. As you stated them, they were much more puzzling. I didn't understand that tale of the dog going in and out of the water; it didn't seem to me a doggy thing to do. If Nox had been very much upset about something else, he might possibly have refused to go after the stick at all. He'd probably go off nosing in whatever direction he suspected the mischief. But when once a dog is actually chasing a thing, a stone or a stick or a rabbit, my experience is that he won't stop for anything but the most peremptory command, and not always for that. That he should turn round because his mood changed seems to me unthinkable."

"But he did turn round," insisted Fiennes; "and came back without the stick."

"He came back without the stick for the best reason in the world," replied the priest. "He came back because he couldn't find it. He whined because he couldn't find it. That's the sort of thing a dog really does whine about. A dog is a devil of a ritualist. He is as particular about the precise routine of a game as a child about the precise repetition of a fairy-tale. In this case something had gone wrong with the game. He came back to complain seriously of the conduct of the stick. Never had such a thing happened before. Never had an eminent and distinguished dog been so treated by a rotten old walking-stick."

"Why, what had the walking-stick done?" inquired the young man.

"It had sunk," said Father Brown.

Fiennes said nothing, but continued to stare; and it was the priest who continued:

"It had sunk because it was not really a stick, but a rod of steel with a very thin shell of cane and a sharp point. In other words, it was a sword-stick. I suppose a murderer never gets rid of a bloody weapon so oddly and yet so naturally as by throwing it into the sea for a retriever."

"I begin to see what you mean," admitted Fiennes; "but even if a sword-stick was used, I have no guess of how it was used."

"I had a sort of guess," said Father Brown, "right at the beginning when you said the word summer-house. And another when you said that Druce wore a white coat. As long as everybody was looking for a short dagger, nobody thought of it; but if we admit a rather long blade like a rapier, it's not so impossible."

He was leaning back, looking at the ceiling, and began like one going back to his own first thoughts and fundamentals.

"All that discussion about detective stories like the Yellow Room, about a man found dead in sealed chambers which no one could enter, does not apply to the present case, because it is a summer-house. When we talk of a Yellow Room, or any room, we imply walls that are really homogeneous and impenetrable. But a summer-house is not made like that; it is often made, as it was in this case, of closely interlaced but separate boughs and strips of wood, in which there are chinks here and there. There was one of them just behind Druce's back as he sat in his chair up against the wall. But just as the room was a summer-house, so the chair was a basket-chair. That also was a lattice of loopholes. Lastly, the summer-house was close up under the hedge; and you have just told me that it was really a thin hedge. A man standing outside it could easily see, amid a network of twigs and branches and canes, one white spot of the Colonel's coat as plain as the white of a target.

"Now, you left the geography a little vague; but it was possible to put two and two together. You said the Rock of Fortune was not really high; but you also said it could be seen dominating the garden like a mountain-peak. In other words, it was very near the end of the garden, though your walk had taken you a long way round to it. Also, it isn't likely the young lady really howled so as to be heard half a mile. She gave an ordinary involuntary cry, and yet you heard it on the shore. And among other interesting things that you told me, may I remind you that you said Harry Druce had fallen behind to light his pipe under a hedge."

Fiennes shuddered slightly. "You mean he drew his blade there and sent it through the hedge at the white spot. But surely it was a very odd chance and a very sudden choice. Besides, he couldn't be certain the old man's money had passed to him, and as a fact it hadn't."

Father Brown's face became animated.

"You misunderstand the man's character," he said, as if he himself had known the man all his life. "A curious but not unknown type of character. If he had really *known* the money would come to him, I seriously believe he wouldn't have done it. He would have seen it as the dirty thing it was."

"Isn't that rather paradoxical?" asked the other.

"This man was a gambler," said the priest, "and a man in disgrace for having taken risks and anticipated orders. It was probably for something pretty unscrupulous, for every imperial police is more like a Russian secret police than we like to think. But he had gone beyond the line and failed. Now, the temptation of that type of man is to do a mad thing precisely because the risk will be wonderful in retrospect. He wants to say, 'Nobody but I could have seized that chance or seen that it was then or never. What a wild and wonderful guess it was, when I put all those things together; Donald in disgrace; and the lawyer being sent for; and Herbert and I sent for at the same time—and then nothing more but the way the old man grinned at me and shook hands. Anybody would say I was mad to risk it; but that is how fortunes are made, by the man mad enough to have a little foresight.' In short, it is the vanity of guessing. It is the megalomania of the gambler. The more incongruous the coincidence, the more instantaneous the decision, the more likely he is to snatch the chance. The accident, the very triviality of the white speck and the hole in the hedge intoxicated him like a vision of the world's desire. Nobody clever enough to see such a combination of accidents could be cowardly enough not to use them! That is how the devil talks to the gambler. But the devil himself would hardly have induced that unhappy man to go down in a dull, deliberate way and kill an old uncle from whom he'd always had expectations. It would be too respectable."

He paused a moment, and then went on with a certain quiet emphasis.

"And now try to call up the scene, even as you saw it yourself. As he stood there, dizzy with his diabolical opportunity, he looked up and saw that strange outline that might have been the image of his own tottering soul; the one great crag poised perilously on the other like a pyramid on its point, and remembered that it was called the Rock of Fortune. Can you guess how such a man at such a moment would read such a signal? I think it strung him up to action and even to vigilance. He who would be a tower must not fear to be a toppling tower. Anyhow, he acted; his next difficulty was to cover his tracks. To be found with a sword-stick, let alone a bloodstained sword-stick, would be fatal in the search that was certain to follow. If he left it anywhere, it would be found and probably traced. Even if he threw it into the sea the action might be noticed, and thought noticeable—unless indeed he could think of some more natural way of covering the action. As you know, he did think of one, and a very good one. Being the only one of you with a watch, he told you it was not yet time to return, strolled a little farther and started the game of throwing in sticks for the retriever. But how his eyes must have rolled darkly over all that desolate sea-shore before they alighted on the dog!"

Fiennes nodded, gazing thoughtfully into space. His mind seemed to have drifted back to a less practical part of the narrative.

"It's queer," he said, "that the dog really was in the story after all."

"The dog could almost have told you the story, if he could talk," said the priest. "All I complain of is that because he couldn't talk, you made up his story for him, and made him talk with the tongues of men and angels. It's part of something I've noticed more and more in the modern world, appearing in all sorts of newspaper rumours and conversational catchwords; something that's arbitrary without being authoritative. People readily swallow the untested claims of this, that, or the other.

It's drowning all your old rationalism and scepticism, it's coming in like a sea; and the name of it is superstition." He stood up abruptly, his face heavy with a sort of frown, and went on talking almost as if he were alone. "It's the first effect of not believing in God that you lose your common sense and can't see things as they are. Anything that anybody talks about, and says there's a good deal in it, extends itself indefinitely like a vista in a nightmare. And a dog is an omen, and a cat is a mystery, and a pig is a mascot and a beetle is a scarab, calling up all the menagerie of polytheism from Egypt and old India; Dog Anubis and great green-eyed Pasht and all the holy howling Bulls of Bashan; reeling back to the bestial gods of the beginning, escaping into elephants and snakes and crocodiles; and all because you are frightened of four words: 'He was made Man'."

The young man got up with a little embarrassment, almost as if he had overheard a soliloquy. He called to the dog and left the room with vague but breezy farewells. But he had to call the dog twice, for the dog had remained behind quite motionless for a moment, looking up steadily at Father Brown as the wolf looked at St Francis.

THE CLEANERS
by Michael Gilbert

Born in England in 1912, Michael Gilbert was a partner in a London law firm until his retirement a few years ago. He published his first novel, Close Quarters, *in 1947 and did much of his subsequent writing on the daily train rides between London and his home in Kent. Thus far he has produced some two dozen novels and five collections of short stories, as well as numerous plays for the stage, radio and television. In May of 1987 he received the Grand Master award, the highest honor from the Mystery Writers of America.*

Though most of Michael Gilbert's novels have been without a series character (the exceptions are six early books about Inspector Hazelrigg, shown at his best in the 1950 classic Smallbone Deceased) *Gilbert seems to prefer series sleuths in his shorter works. The espionage stories about Mr. Calder and Mr. Behrens are among the best in their field, comparing favorably with the Ashenden stories of W. Somerset Maugham. And the police procedurals featuring Detective Inspector Patrick Petrella, officer in charge of the Patton Street police station in South London, give a realistic view of everyday crime from the police viewpoint. In this story, the only novella Gilbert has written about Petrella, the world of London's professional criminals seems a long way from the vicar's rose garden of so many other British mysteries.*

"The Cleaners" first appeared in the 1977 collection Petrella at Q.

Part I

Inquest on the Death of Bernie Nicholls

"Say it after me," said the Coroner's officer, eyeing the jury as a drill-sergeant might eye a batch of recruits. "I will diligently enquire into and a true presentment make—" The jury did its best. "Of all matters given into our charge concerning the death of Bernard Francis Nicholls. And will without fear or favour a true verdict give according to the evidence produced before us"—"According to the evidence," said a bright-looking girl, three beats behind the choir and in a very clear voice, "produced before us."

The Coroner's officer looked at her suspiciously and replaced the printed card on the shelf in front of the jury box. The Coroner said, "Well now—" and Police Sergeant Underhill of the Thames Division of the Metropolitan Police took the oath and explained to the Coroner that, being on duty on the morning of January 1st, he had been passing Malvern Steps and had observed what appeared to him to be a body lying on the foreshore below the Malvern Jetty and just above the high-water mark.

"What time of day was this, Sergeant?"

"Approximately half past seven, sir. Just beginning to get light."

The Coroner made a note. He was a nice little man and Petrella, who was at the back waiting to be called in the next case, knew him for a breeder of canaries and an unreliable bridge player. A sound enough Coroner, though, who went by the book when it suited him and stood no nonsense.

"I directed the police launch to the steps and climbed down onto the foreshore. I found the body of a man lying head downwards, that is to say with his head towards the water. Since he had quite clearly been dead for some time I did not disturb the body. I observed a broken portion of wooden railing near the body and I saw that there was a break in the railing which ran along the edge of the quay about six feet above him. I therefore deduced—"

"That's all right," said the Coroner. "You thought he'd fallen through the railing, very probably he had."

A man, with thick black hair and a thick white face, rose to his feet, said, "The point will be disputed, sir," and sat down again.

The Coroner said, "Good gracious. Mr Tasker. I didn't see you. Do you appear in this case?"

"I represent Mr Mablethorpe, the owner of the premises and of the quay," said Mr Tasker.

"And I represent the deceased," said a thin, sad-looking man.

The Coroner peered at the second speaker over the top of his glasses, identified him, and said, "Very well, Mr Lampe. Some dispute about liability, no doubt. Looks as though we shall be here for some time. I expect that's all you can really tell us, isn't it, Sergeant? Any evidence of identity?"

Mr Lampe rose once more to his feet and said, "I am able to identify the body. The man was employed in my office and his name—"

"Better have this formally. For the record, you know."

Mr Lampe accordingly moved from his seat on the solicitors' bench to the witness box and told the court that he identified the deceased as Bernard Francis Nicholls aged fifty and employed by his firm, Messrs. Gidney, Lampe and Glazier, as a legal assistant.

"Not a qualified solicitor?"

"No sir. But a very experienced conveyancing clerk. He had been with us for five years."

"When did you see him last, Mr Lampe?"

"When I left the office at about six o'clock on the night of December 31st."

The Coroner's officer said, "There is a witness who saw him later that evening."

"Very well," said the Coroner. "But let's hear the

doctor first. I'm sure he wants to get away. Doctors always do."

Doctor Pond said that he had examined the body, both *in situ* and later at the Kentledge Road Mortuary. There were minor abrasions, consistent with a fall from the quay on to the foreshore, a distance of about six feet. There was also one large depressed fracture, on the crown of the head, a little right of centre. He placed his own hand on top of his head to demonstrate the position. The Coroner nodded and said, "He could have hit his head, I suppose, when he fell."

Dr Pond said, cautiously, that there were several large stones embedded in the mud of the foreshore and he understood that the police had removed one of them for further examination.

"Yes, doctor?"

"I examined the contents of the stomach," said Dr Pond, with the relish with which pathologists always seem to discuss this topic, "and I discovered what appeared to be the remains of a meal taken shortly before death consisting principally of ham and bread. It was also apparent that the deceased had consumed a substantial quantity of whisky in the last hours of his life. There was evidence, from the degeneration of the liver and the spleen, that this indulgence may not have been of recent origin."

Observing the jury looking baffled, the Coroner said helpfully, "That's the doctor's way of saying that he had been a heavy drinker for some time. Would you have said an alcoholic, doctor?"

"It would be difficult to be certain."

"And in your opinion the blow on the head was the cause of death."

Dr Pond hesitated for a moment and then said, "It was certainly one of the causes."

"One of the causes?"

"It is possible that the blow on the head rendered him unconscious and that the proximate cause of death was exposure. You will bear in mind, sir, that the night of December 31st was a very cold one. There was a short fall of snow around midnight and there was snow actually on the body when I saw it."

The Coroner said, "Yes, I see," and the jury tried to look as though there was some point which they ought to be thinking about. "Were you able to arrive at any conclusion as to the time of death?"

"In the circumstances it was not easy to be definite. But when I saw the deceased at nine o'clock that morning I judged that he had been dead at least eight hours. More probably ten or twelve."

The young lady juror said, "If there was snow on the body and none underneath it, it would mean that he was there before the snow started at midnight, surely."

"That would be a logical conclusion," said the Coroner blandly. "Thank you, doctor."

The next witness, a big red-faced bald-headed man said that his name was Saul Elder, and that he was licensee of the Wheelwrights Arms in Sutton Street. He knew the deceased well by sight. He regularly patronised the Wheelwrights Arms and had been there on the night in question. He had eaten two rounds of ham sandwich and had consumed three double and two single whiskies.

"Was that a normal evening's intake?"

Mr Elder said that it varied. Sometimes Mr Nicholls drank more than that. Sometimes less. It was about average. He had left about eleven o'clock.

"Did he seem to be in normal spirits when he left?"

For a moment Petrella, who knew Mr Elder well, thought that he was going to make some gruesome play on the word spirits, but he evidently recollected where he was and confined himself to saying that Mr Nicholls looked much as usual.

The last witness was Detective Chief Inspector Loveday, in whose manor Malvern Steps lay. (A hundred yards downstream and it would have been Petrella's headache.) He said that he had been called to the scene at half past eight. Some photographs had been taken, which he could produce. He had taken charge of a large piece of stone and had submitted it to the Forensic Science Laboratory. He could also produce their report. The point of interest in it was that they had found a quantity of blood on the stone, and embedded in the blood some small splinters of bone. The blood was of the same group as the deceased and the splinters were quite clearly from his skull.

The Coroner said, "The jury can see the photographs if they wish. But I don't imagine that they add anything to your evidence, Inspector."

The witness agreed and said that the jury might find some of them a bit unpleasant. The foreman, after collecting nods, said he thought they could arrive at a verdict without seeing the photographs.

Inspector Loveday was about to step down when it was observed that Mr Tasker was on his feet. He said, "Tell me, Inspector, was one of them a photograph of the broken piece of railing we heard about?"

"Yes."

"Of the railing itself?"

"Yes."

"I'd like the jury to see that one."

"Perhaps you have a spare copy for me," said the Coroner.

Spare copies were produced with such speed that Petrella guessed that Loveday must have been warned what to expect.

Mr Tasker said, "I'd like you to observe that the railing is comparatively new, and is formed of stout upright posts, approximately five inches square, set in concrete. The railings themselves are bars of wood four inches by three. I shall be calling Mr Mablethorpe who will tell you that it was erected, under his personal supervision, less than two years ago. The wood is oak, which is not—" here Mr Tasker bared a fine set of white teeth, "a notably fragile material."

"I've no doubt it was a very fine fence," said the Coroner. "But the fact is that one of the bars broke."

"Quite so," said Mr Tasker. "The question is, who broke it, and how did they do it?"

It was extraordinary, thought Petrella, how the whole atmosphere of the court had suddenly changed. The jury were no longer apathetic, but were crowding together to look at the photographs. The Coroner had his head on one side, like a blackbird sighting a promising worm. His colleague, Jack Loveday, was looking resigned.

"I would ask the jury," said Mr Tasker, "to look particularly at the first photograph. A very good and detailed photograph, if I may say so. They will observe three overlapping circular depressions, of approximately four inches in diameter, close to the fractured end of the rail. It is not easy to judge from the photograph, but I have been allowed to examine the railing itself, and I can assure them that they vary from a quarter to a full third of an inch in depth. In my view they were made by a very heavy sledge-hammer, applied with considerable force—"

"Well," said Loveday, "he got his adjournment, which is what he was angling for. The rail and post have gone up to the lab for a report."

"What's it all about," said Petrella. They were having a quick beer at the pub opposite the court.

"He came in originally to look after old Mablethorpe's interests. If the fence had been rotten, there could have been a hefty claim for damages by Nicholls's wife. Now he's seen the photographs he's taking it a lot farther."

"Yes," said Petrella. He knew Mr Tasker for a man who never left a promising hare unhunted. "But what exactly is in his mind?"

"I wish you'd find out," said Loveday. "You know him better than I do, and his office is nearer you than me."

Petrella, who was aware that Loveday was involved in a particularly unpleasant child-murder case said, "All right. I'll take it on and let you know what happens. O.K.?"

"O.K." said Loveday. "And thank you."

Mr Tasker ran a one-man solicitor's practice from an office near the Oval. He appeared in the local Magistrates' Courts indiscriminately for and against the police. Petrella had found him to be astute, but fair, in both rôles.

He said, "I saw you at the back of the court, Inspector. I guessed you might be round to see me."

"I wanted to hear a bit more about this railing."

"Have a look at this sketch. It'll show you the point I was trying to make. The end of each rail was countersunk into the post on the *inner* side. You see what that means?"

"It means that it couldn't have been knocked off by someone falling against it. The top of the post would be in the way. Right?"

"Correct. And each rail is fastened to the post by

three six-inch nails driven right through and turned flat on the other side. You won't shift them in a hurry."

"Then the only alternative is a flaw in the wooden rail."

"Right," said Mr Tasker. "That's the only alternative. But in this case it isn't true. I've had the rail examined by my own expert. He'll say that it's as sound a piece of oak as you'll find anywhere in England."

The two men looked at each other in silence for several seconds. Then Petrella said, "So what's your idea about all this?"

"I think it's fairly obvious."

"Let's have it, all the same."

"Someone wanted Nicholls out of the way. It was more than one person probably. It's got the feel of a gang job. All they had to do was follow him home from the pub. They knew he'd go past Malvern Steps and they knew he'd be full of whisky. One of them has already got hold of a handy chunk of rock from the foreshore. He walks up behind him, and slugs him on top of the head with it. Didn't it strike you as odd that the fracture should have been on *top* of his head. If you broke through a railing and fell six feet you might land on your face or you might land on your bottom, but you wouldn't land on top of your head."

"It did strike me as a bit odd," said Petrella. "You suggest they just pitched him down and put the chunk of rock back beside him. And broke the rail and threw that down too."

"That's right. And that rail took some breaking. They had to hit it three times with a fourteen-pound sledge-hammer to crack it."

"Can you think of any reason why anyone should want to get rid of Nicholls?"

"Search me."

"Did you know him professionally?"

"We were sometimes on opposite sides in a house sale or purchase. He acted for Lloyds."

Petrella was aware that in that part of South London if someone mentioned Lloyds they meant neither the well-known City outfit nor the bank. They were referring to Lloyd and Lloyd who were the largest and busiest local firm of property dealers specialising in sales of small houses, flats and one-man businesses. Petrella knew them well. He had bought his own flat from them.

Mr Tasker said, "Nicholls brought them all the Lloyds business. He knew old Jimmy Lloyd from army days. Now Nicholls has gone, the business will go somewhere else. Lampe's got no one capable of handling it."

"Hasn't he got any partners? What about Gidney and Glazier?"

"Gidney's dead. Glazier's retired. Lampe ought to have retired too. Probably can't afford to. Poor old sod."

A more cheerful aspect of the matter occurred to Mr Tasker. He said, "Come to think of it, if he loses Lloyds' business, I might get it."

"You realise that makes you the number one suspect," said Petrella. As he was going he added, "If you do hear anything about Nicholls, you might pass it on and we'll look into it. It'll help you to get the verdict you want if you can suggest some sort of motive."

"You scratch my back, I'll scratch yours," said Mr Tasker cheerfully.

The offices of Messrs Gidney, Lampe and Glazier were in Kentledge Road, opposite the mortuary. There was a sad air of mortality about them, too, the unmistakable odour of decay.

Mr Lampe received Petrella in a room which was lined on one side with deed boxes and on two sides with books. Neither boxes nor books looked as though they had been opened for some years. Mr Lampe said, "I saw you in court, Inspector. Do I understand that you are now in charge of this matter?"

"I'm giving Inspector Loveday a hand," said Petrella. "Temporarily. I thought you might be able to tell me something about Nicholls."

"Ah," said Mr Lampe. "Yes. Well—he was a very able conveyancer. Before he came to me he had been many years with a firm in Lincoln's Inn. But he found the daily journey across London tiring. As we grow older, Inspector, bodily comfort becomes more and more important."

"He was a native of these parts."

"He has lived here all his life. And married a local girl. I am doing what I can to look after her, poor soul."

"Is she hard up?"

This direct question seemed to disconcert Mr Lampe. He said, "You'll understand that I haven't had time to look closely into Nicholls's private affairs. But I never got the impression that he had a great deal of money to spare."

"It would seem," said Petrella, "that any money he did have to spare went on whisky."

"I find that remark uncalled for."

"When you took him on, did you *know* that he was an alcoholic?"

A flush spread over Mr Lampe's pale face. He said, "There is no truth in that at all. I was surprised that the Coroner let the question stand. I shall take the first opportunity at the adjourned hearing to protest very strongly. Mr Nicholls liked a drink after the day's work was over. If that makes him an alcoholic, there must be a great number of them about—"

"I'm afraid I put the old boy's back up," said Petrella

to Sergeant Roughead. "A pity, because after that he stood on his professional dignity and I couldn't get anything out of him at all. We shall have to tackle this from the other end. You'd better go along and have a word with Saul Elder at the Wheelwrights. I'd like to know who Nicholls was drinking with that evening."

Sergeant Milo Roughead, late of Eton and the ranks of the Metropolitan Constabulary, accepted the assignment with enthusiasm. He had always found Mr Elder friendly, and drinking in pursuit of information was the sort of duty which appealed to him.

The Wheelwrights Arms, though full to suffocation on most evenings, was little patronised by day. He found the saloon bar empty and Mr Elder, with his sleeves rolled up, polishing glasses. He drew a pint for Milo and a half pint for himself and said, "And what may we do to help the cause of law and order, Sergeant?"

"You can tell me something. Who was here with Nicholls on the night he was killed?"

When Mr Elder froze into sudden immobility, Milo realised that he might have been indiscreet. There was a long silence. Then Mr Elder slowly resumed his polishing. It was a full minute before he said, "Killed, eh? So that's what Tasker was getting at. I thought it might be."

He examined the glass, holding it up against the light, then put it down and picked up another one.

"It's not certain, by any means," said Milo. "But we're looking at it that way for the moment."

"So you want to know who was drinking with Nicholls?"

"That's right."

"Difficult to say. He had a lot of friends. Not friends really. Acquaintances. People who would always take a drink off him, and sometimes stand him one back. Charlie Cousins, the bookmaker. Phil Green, who drives a taxi. You know him. Sam—I don't know his other name—works in the Goods Depot. I could give you a half dozen names if I thought hard enough. They was all in here that night, and more besides. We had an extension up to midnight, seeing as how it was New Year's Eve."

"But you don't remember any one in particular?"

"No. First one, then the other."

"Did anyone leave with him?"

Mr Elder thought hard about this. Whilst he was thinking the door of the small bar at the back opened and two men came out. Milo could see them quite clearly in the mirror behind the bar. Both of them were big men, who carried themselves like soldiers. Both had the pug faces of fighters, short noses, small eyes and unobtrusive ears. The one in front had smooth black hair. The other had thick reddish hair which grew to a peak on his forehead and ran down either side of his face in long side-boards.

They walked out without speaking and the street door swung softly shut behind them.

"I got a few names," said Milo, "and I can check up on them, but I don't fancy we shall get much out of them. It was a New Year's Eve crush, everyone standing drinks to everyone else. There was one thing, though. Did we ever connect the Wheelwrights with the crowd from the Elephant—Les Congdon's lot?"

"The Elephant? No, I don't think so. They usually stick to their own patch of the jungle."

There had been a dynasty of gangs centred on the Elephant and Castle; known at different times as the Elephant boys, the Mahoots or the Jumbos—or simply by the name of the man who happened to have taken over the leadership. They were the mercenary soldiers of the South Bank, happy to sell their services to the best paymaster; dispersed when some gross outrage had roused the police to action; re-forming as soon as the dust had settled.

"Why do you ask?"

"I thought I spotted two of them coming out of the private bar. Chris Mason, I'm sure was one of them. I recognised that widow's peak.

"If that's right," said Petrella, "the black-haired one was probably his brother, Len."

"They didn't look like brothers."

"Their father was Buster Mason who used to box at the Blackfriars Ring. He was married four times—officially. Died of a brain hemorrhage some years ago. Chris and Len are bad boys. I'll have a word with Loveday. They're his homework, not mine." He was wrapping a scarf round his neck as he spoke and buttoning up his raincoat. The weather was vile. Rain alternating with sleet, driven by a wind which was blowing from the North Sea. "I'm going to have a word with Jimmy Lloyd. Private business. You can look after the shop until I get back."

James Lloyd was sixty-five. The years since the ending of the war had brought him a lot of money. They had also added unnecessary pounds to his weight, an inflated paunch and a troublesome digestion. It was hard to believe that he had once played wing-threequarter for Aberavon.

He said, "Shouldn't be too difficult to find a buyer. Everyone's looking for small flats. You'll be after something bigger, I take it?"

"We'll need one more room at least," said Petrella, "when the second child does decide to put in an appearance. Preferably a spare room as well."

"Two living, three beds, usual offices." Mr Lloyd

made a note on his pad. "What did you put down when you bought this one?"

"I paid seven hundred pounds for a gas-stove, two tatty carpets and some pelmets which we pulled down as soon as we got in."

"Usual swindle," said Mr Lloyd. "Much more honest to call it a premium and have done with it. You didn't throw the pelmets away, I hope."

"We've got them stowed away somewhere. *And* we've put in a new gas-stove."

"Lovely," said Mr Lloyd. "Present state of the market, should be able to get you a thousand. Of course, you'll have to lay most of it out again when you get a new flat. Tom Adams will keep his eyes open too. Right, Tom?"

This was to a tiny, bird-like man who had come into the room without knocking.

"My head accountant, Tom Adams," said Mr Lloyd. "I don't think you know Detective Chief Inspector Petrella, do you?"

"I haven't had the pleasure," said Mr Adams in a thin piping voice.

"The Inspector wants to move into a larger flat. Three beds. Must do our best for him. Got to keep on the right side of the law, boy."

Mr Adams looked doubtful. He said, "It's a very popular size. I'll certainly keep my eyes open." He paused. "If you're busy now, I can easily come back."

"That's all right," said Petrella. "I've finished."

When he got back to Patton Street Station he sent for Detective Sergeant Ambrose, and said, "There's a job I want you to look into. It was a long firm fraud. About ten years ago up at Highside. I've forgotten the name of the man concerned. It wasn't my case. He was an unqualified accountant who worked for a firm of builders.

Sent down for five years by Arbuthnot at the Bailey. See if you can find me the name and a photograph."

Sergeant Ambrose accepted this vague assignment calmly. He was a painstaking and methodical person and had no doubt that he could unearth the information without too much difficulty.

The inquest on Nicholls was resumed a fortnight later. Photographs and reports were produced to the jury. Mr Lampe's strong protest about the description of the deceased as an alcoholic was duly noted. The Press, who had been alerted to the possibilities of the case, were there in force. The Coroner summed up at length and the jury, after discussion, returned a disappointing verdict; that there was insufficient evidence to show how Bernard Francis Nicholls had come to his death.

Chief Superintendent Watterson, at Division, read the report of the inquest and said to Petrella, "I suppose you'd better keep the file open. Something might turn up." Which was as good as saying, "Forget about it and get on with your own work. You've got plenty of other things to do."

A week later Nicholls was cremated, the principal mourners being his wife, who seemed to be bearing up reasonably well, and a sister who came down from Lancashire for the occasion. Mr Lampe made the arrangements and attended the ceremony.

On the following day Petrella heard the good news. Mr Lloyd had found a flat for him. He went round with his wife to see it and they both liked it. It had three bedrooms and a large cupboard which could, with imagination, be described as a fourth bedroom. Mr Lloyd said, "Had a bit of luck there. Man who lived in it is working for the Electricity Board. He's been moved up to Scotland. Got to get out quick. Prepared to take five hundred."

A week later Petrella was installed in his new flat and had received the sum of four hundred and twenty-five pounds, in notes, from Mr Lloyd, this being the difference between the thousand pounds which he had duly got for the gas-cooker, two threadbare carpets and the hastily re-fixed pelmets, the five hundred he had paid for an electric water-heater and an old sofa in the new flat, and Mr Lloyd's commission on the double deal.

It was on a Monday, a week after the move, that Sergeant Ambrose laid a photograph on Petrella's desk. He said, "I think this is the man you were enquiring after, sir. Named Thomas Anderson. Five years for fraudulent trading. Twelve other cases taken into consideration. Released after serving three years and four months. Nothing known since."

They were clear photographs, taken from the front and in both profiles. There was not the least doubt that it was Tom Adams, head cashier at Lloyd and Lloyd.

Petrella gave the matter a lot of thought. On the one hand, he had personal reasons for feeling grateful to Mr Lloyd. On the other hand, it looked as though Adams had been going straight since he came out of gaol. If he did say anything to Lloyd, and Adams lost his job, would he not be guilty of persecuting an innocent man who had fought his way back from crime to respectability? It was the twelve other cases that made him hesitate. Could a man who had committed such a systematic series of frauds ever really be trusted to look after someone else's money?

It was while he was thinking about it that the telephone rang. It was Superintendent Watterson. He said, "You're wanted at District tomorrow at ten o'clock."

"What on earth for?"

"No idea," said Watterson. "But you'd better brush

your hair and put on a clean collar. It's the old man who wants to see you."

The head of C.I.D. in No. 2 District, at that time, was Commander Baylis. He was not popular with his subordinates, although he seemed to satisfy his superiors well enough. He had come to his appointment through the specialised branches at Central, having risen from the Criminal Record Office, via control of the Fraud Squad to a quiet Division on the respectable western fringe of London. Watterson had once described him to Petrella, in an unguarded moment, as an old woman. Petrella's occasional encounters with him had done nothing to dispel this impression.

When he was shown into the Commander's office he was surprised to see a third man, whom he recognised from past dealings over pension contributions, as Mr Rose, an assistant in the office of the secretary.

Baylis said, "Sit down, sit down. I'm sorry to drag you all the way up here, but a point has come up on which I thought I ought to have a word with you personally."

The words were polite enough, but Petrella felt a faint tremor of disquiet.

"Perhaps you'd be good enough to explain to the Inspector, Mr Rose."

Mr Rose said, "As you know, Inspector, we go to great lengths to monitor the bank accounts of police officers. The commonest form of attack, by people who want to get the police into trouble, is to suggest that illicit payments have been made to them, very often directly into their bank accounts."

Petrella said, "Yes." He was aware of the system. Like all police officers of a certain seniority he had signed an authority to his own bank opening his account to inspection.

"We made one of our periodical checks on your own account yesterday. You had paid in a rather large sum, in notes. Four hundred and twenty-five pounds."

Petrella said, the relief in his voice evident to the two men, "That's quite all right. It was a balance which was due to me when I changed flats, apparently two bedroom ones are more saleable than three bedroom ones. You can check it all up with Lloyd and Lloyd."

Mr Rose looked at Commander Baylis who said, "Yes, yes. I see. That explains how the money came into your hands. It doesn't explain why thirty of the ten-pound notes were part of the proceeds of a recent wage snatch."

Part II

A Lively Night at Basildon Mansions

When he had got his breath back, Petrella said, "Which particular wage snatch was that, sir?"

"At Corinth Car Parts. Last November."

"Two months ago."

"Fourteen months ago."

Petrella nearly said, "I should hardly describe that as recent." It was the sort of thing he would have said to Watterson without a second thought. Something told him that Baylis might not take it well. Mr Rose, obedient to a slight inclination of the head, had slid out of the room.

Baylis said, "You may be excused for not knowing much about it, Inspector. For better or worse, it was handed over to the Serious Crimes Squad. And we all know the secrecy with which the S.C.S. like to wrap up *their* operations."

Petrella did know it. He was also beginning to understand the acrimony in Baylis's voice.

Since their formation two years before, the Serious

Crimes Squad had done a lot of good work. They had also upset the regular hierarchy of the C.I.D.; a hierarchy which linked the Detective on the job, the Detective Inspector in charge of the Station, the Detective Superintendent or Chief Superintendent at Division and the Commander at District in an orderly and well-understood chain of command. The S.C.S. by-passed all of these and was answerable only to the Assistant Commissioner at Central. Districts and Divisions were given periodical reports of their operations, but had no executive control over them.

Petrella said, "How much did they get?"

"Ninety thousand pounds. Corinth is a big outfit, but it wouldn't have been anything like that if it hadn't been the last week in November, when they hand out the Christmas bonus."

"We had another big one in April," said Petrella. "G.E.X. Engineering in Deptford."

"There have been two since then. G.E.X. was in April. Costa-Cans in September. That adds up to three major unsolved wage snatches in my District. In my opinion—"

What indiscretion Baylis was on the point of committing was not to be revealed. Mr Rose had sidled back into the room. He nodded his head.

Petrella knew what he had been doing. He had been telephoning Lloyd and Lloyd and checking up on his story. He took no umbrage. He would have done the same in Baylis's place.

"Although we aren't allowed to interfere in an S.C.S. operation," said Baylis, "I hardly think the powers that be could object to your following up an obvious lead of this sort, do you?"

The atmosphere had become noticeably more friendly.

"I certainly think I ought to follow it up, sir. After all, we don't know that it had anything to do with the Corinth job. The money may have passed through half a dozen hands. It's simply a case of a firm being found in possession of stolen property. A routine enquiry."

"Exactly," said Baylis. "They can't expect *all* detective work in the District to come to a grinding halt just because the S.C.S. has been engaged—and not too successfully engaged if I might say so—in investigations in our manor, can they?"

"I've got the reports here, if you'd like to look at them," said Watterson. "Most of the banknotes taken in the Corinth job were ordinary small denomination stuff, used notes, impossible to trace. It was just that the directors thought it would be a nice idea to give each of their senior employees a ten-pound note in their bonus packet. They were the new Florence Nightingale issue. So they drew this packet of two hundred tenners and the bank kept a note of the serial numbers which were in sequence. It's thirty of those notes that have ended up in your pocket. It doesn't prove anything against Lloyds of course. Most of their transactions are on a cash basis. Sale of small businesses and stock-in-trade, as well as flats and houses."

"I imagine the Inspector of Taxes would like a sight of their books."

"They don't keep books. They keep a bank account. The money goes in one end and out at the other. All the same, Mr Lloyd might be able to help. It can't be every day that he gets paid in new ten-pound notes. Why don't you ask him?"

"I'd do just that," said Petrella. "I'm not sure that he could tell us."

"Oh?"

"The man who looks after the cash is a Mr Adams."

"Then ask him."

"That might be counter-productive," said Petrella. He told Watterson about Mr Adams, alias Anderson. Watterson scratched his pointed chin and said, "I see. Yes. This begins to have an interesting sort of smell about it. If Adams *is* bent, do you think someone might be using him to dispose of some of their hot money?"

"It seemed possible. The only thing is, if it's right, ought we to tackle it ourselves?"

Watterson said, in almost exactly the same tones as Baylis, "The S.C.S. can't expect us to suspend all work in the Division just because they've got interested in two or three jobs round here."

"Actually," said Petrella, "couldn't we have handled those jobs just as well as the S.C.S.?"

"I'm not sure," said Watterson. "I don't get as up-tight about it as Fred Baylis. Those three snatches were real professional efforts. It wasn't so much the snatch itself. That was a case of using plenty of muscle. Hitting hard and running fast. All very tightly planned no doubt, but there've been plenty of others as good. It was the intelligence work that was outstanding. They've always struck when there was a maximum of money available. In the G.E.X. case in April they were actually paying out a three weeks' supplement, all in one go, on the settlement of a round of wage bargaining. In the Costa-Cans case the company knew that it was a heavy pay-out that week and took special precautions. The security team went to the bank in their usual van and collected a dummy pay-roll. Satchels full of old newspapers, actually. The real money went out of the back door of the bank in a private car. *That* was the car they hit. You can see what I mean by organisation. It's all in the reports. Take them away and read them."

As Petrella was going he said, "Who was that expensive-looking lady in the expensive-looking car that I saw waiting outside District Headquarters?"

"That," said Watterson, "would be Mrs Baylis. A second reason for Fred's ulcers."

Petrella said, "We've got a job on, and it's going to need very careful handling, because there are a lot of toes that haven't got to be trodden on."

His audience consisted of Detective Sergeant Blencowe, large and impassive; Detective Sergeant Milo Roughead, tall and dressed in a manner nicely calculated to compromise between a country house upbringing and life in the ranks of the C.I.D., Detective Sergeant Ambrose (looking his normal neat and efficient self), and probationary Detective Lampier, recently promoted to the plain-clothes branch and looking, if it were possible, even more untidy out of uniform than he had looked in it.

"Another thing," said Petrella, "this is something outside the ordinary day-by-day stuff. We can't have routine entirely disrupted by it. It'll have to be tackled as and when we can manage it. Along with all our other stuff."

His audience tried to look enthusiastic. Only Detective Lampier succeeded convincingly. He was new to the job.

"What we want to find out is whether there's any connection between Lloyd and Lloyd and the villains who pulled these three snatches. You can be certain that if there *is* any connection it's carefully organised. These aren't the sort of people who leave letters lying around or make incautious telephone calls. The way I propose to tackle it, we'll make a two-pronged attack. I've no real reason to think that Lloyd himself is involved, but Blencowe can chat him up and see if he can get anything useful. He knows you used to play for London Welsh and he used to play for Aberavon years ago. It'll make a point of contact."

"I'm not sure that it'll be tactful to remind him," said Blencowe. "When we played Aberavon last year one of their forwards got his ear bitten—mind you, it was his fault, he should have kept his ears to himself."

"Why not bite Lloyd in the ear," said Petrella. "It should break the ice beautifully. The rest of you concentrate on Adams. He's the real lead. We've got a friend with an upstairs room we can use. Lloyds shut at half past five and I imagine Adams is away fairly promptly. You can take it in turns, one evening each. Just follow him. Don't breathe down his neck. All I want to know is, if he goes anywhere except straight home."

When Petrella spoke of a "friend" he meant someone who, without being an informer, was prepared to help the police in small ways, reckoning to have it counted in his favour next time he happened to run into trouble. Mr Grandlund, who lived over his wireless shop opposite the offices of Lloyd and Lloyd, was a friend; and it was in his front room, comfortably seated in a chair opposite the window, with the net curtains drawn, that Sergeant Ambrose spent Tuesday evening and Detective Lampier Wednesday evening.

On neither occasion did the following of Mr Adams present any difficulty. He took a bus from the corner, rode out in it to Blackheath where he had a flat in one of the large houses on the heath, went straight in and turned on the television. The watcher, having been told not to make an all-night job of it, left him to it.

Manfred Tillotson got to his feet, moved over to the circular table in the corner, and poured himself out a drink. He put three fingers of brandy into a tumbler and added an equal quantity of dry ginger-ale and a single cube of ice. All his movements were neat and precise.

Carrying the tumbler, he went out of the room, down the hallway to a door at the end, his feet making no noise on the thick grey carpeting on the floor.

It was a bathroom, and there was a girl lying in the bath with her back to the door. Manfred reflected that you could never really judge a girl's age until she had her clothes off. Dressed in the style she affected, Julie would have passed for sixteen. Undressed, it was clear that she was older, though not, perhaps, very much older.

Hearing the click of the door opening the girl turned her head.

"You should never lie in a strange bath with your back to the door," said Manfred. "There was a man called Smith who finished off three wives, just because they were foolish enough to do that."

The girl blinked at him. She said, "Why did he do it, for God's sake? And how?"

"Why was for the insurance money. How was by putting one arm under their knees and lifting them. Their heads went under and they drowned."

"They must have been daft," said Julie. "If I'd been one of them, do you know what I'd do?"

Manfred took a sip from his drink and stood looking down at her. He said, "I'm sure it would be something original."

"I'd hook out the plug with my foot. All the water would be gone long before I drowned."

Tillotson said, "I wonder why none of the Mrs Smiths thought of that. You'd better get dressed, sweetie. My brother's coming in at six."

"So what?"

"Samuel doesn't entirely approve of our arrangements. He says I'm mixing business with pleasure."

"I could never see what was wrong with that," said Julie. "But then I'm an old-fashioned girl."

"I'll pour you an old-fashioned drink."

They were both finishing their drinks when Samuel Tillotson came in. He was older and greyer than his brother, but with the same thickness in the neck and body and the same length of arm and breadth of shoulder. Julie was more afraid of him than of Manny. She finished her drink quickly and said, "Well, I'll be off."

Samuel followed her out in silence, shut the front door behind her and came back into the room.

"Don't say it," said Manfred.

"Don't say what?" said Samuel.

"That it's a mistake to mix business with pleasure. What will you take?"

"A small whisky and water. With that girl, it might be. You know how she came to us?"

"Through Ma Dalby."

"Right. She arrives from Liverpool. Young and broke. Ma Dalby picks her up. Boards and lodges her. And offers her the usual line of employment."

"Which she accepts."

"For a time. Until it occurs to Ma that she's an intelligent girl. A cut above the average runaway. And happens to have taken a secretarial course in her last year at school. So she offers her to us."

"Where she has given great satisfaction."

"I don't doubt it," said Samuel. "More water, if you don't mind. Satisfaction in the office. Satisfaction in the home."

"Then what are you beefing about?"

Samuel Tillotson tasted his drink again, found it to his satisfaction, and swallowed a mouthful. Then he said,

"You know Ma's routine. She likes to know the real name and real address of her girls. They always give her false ones at first, but she has ways of finding out. With Julie it was easy. She had a suitcase with a twopenny lock. As soon as she was out of the house Ma had it open. There was a packet of letters. From an ex-boy friend. She thought it must have been an ex-boy friend. Some of them were quite—intimate."

"So what," said Manfred. "Girls carry things like that about with them."

Samuel didn't seem to hear him. He was gazing into the heart of his drink. Swirling it round gently and peering at it, as though it had some secret he could unlock. He said, "The letters were all handwritten. One of them was still in its envelope. The name and address on the envelope were typed and the envelope had been torn open so roughly that the stamp and postmark and part of the girl's name were gone. But the address was there. 138 Colefax Road, Liverpool. Ma made a note of it before she put the letter back."

"Well?"

"There is a Colefax Road in Liverpool. But there is no number 138. The numbers go no higher than ninety."

Manfred thought about it. He said, "It doesn't prove anything. Julie would know that Ma liked to have their names and addresses. The other girls would have told her. So she faked up the envelope. Right?"

"That's what I mean by the dangers of mixing business and pleasure," said Samuel. "You're saying that because you want her to be what she says she is. A little Liverpudlian, hungry for money and sex. I can think more dispassionately about her."

"And what does your dispassionate thinking tell you?"

"It tells me that we are up against some very clever people. And it tells me that, with our plans for the fourteenth, this isn't a time when we can afford to be careless. She must be watched."

"I don't mind her being watched. But nothing must be done to her until I am convinced."

Samuel pinched his brother affectionately in the muscles of his forearm. He said, "Dear Manny, no step shall be taken until we are unanimous. As always."

On Thursday evening a wind of near gale force, non-stop from Siberia, was hitting the East End of London, slinging bucketfuls of frozen rain horizontally down the street. Milo Roughead had put on two extra pullovers and brought with him an oilskin coat borrowed from a boating friend.

"Nasty night to be out in," said Mr Grandlund. "I'll get you a cupper. Warm the inner man."

Milo was half-way through the cup of tea when he put it down, snatched up his coat and bolted down the stairs. Mr Adams was on the move.

He was battling down the street, head lowered against the wind. He passed the bus stop. His objective turned out to be the Underground station. Milo gave him fifty yards, then followed him, in time to see him disappearing down the moving staircase. He bought himself a ticket to the end of the Northern Line. The station was an old-fashioned one, with emergency stairs. Milo went down them fast. He could hear a train coming. He reached the platform in time to see Mr Adams get in, two carriages farther up. This suited him well. He jumped in after him. The train was on the Bank switch and was nearly empty. They had reached Essex Road before Mr Adams moved. Fortunately three other people got out with him. They all travelled up in the lift together. When they reached the street Mr Adams and the three other men turned right. Milo turned left and walked away from them. Out of the corner of his eye he saw Mr Adams cross the New North Road and make off up Northampton Street. He reversed smartly and followed.

The weather helped. It was the sort of night in which a pedestrian kept his head down and ploughed steadily forward without much regard to what was happening around him. It was quite a long walk, up Alwyne Road and Willow Road, then left again. His knowledge of London geography told Milo that they must be getting close to Canonbury, that much bombed area which had blossomed into fashion after the war, and was now full of tarted-up Georgian houses and blocks of new and expensive flats.

"He can't be walking for pleasure," said Milo to his sodden feet. "Must be getting somewhere soon." At this moment Mr Adams turned to his left up a shallow flight of steps and disappeared into the building.

Milo slowed down, wiped some of the rain out of his eyes and read, above the doorway, in golden letters, "Basildon Mansions".

What now?

There was no sign of the porter. Presumably he was down in his own snug basement with his nose glued to the television and a glass of something in his hand, lucky sod.

Through the glass of the swing door Milo could see a board with the numbers of the flats and the names of their occupants. There were twelve flats, starting with 1a and 1b on the ground floor and running up to 6a and 6b. It was clearly out of the question to knock on twelve different doors and if he waited in the hall he was going to be much too conspicuous when Mr Adams finished his business and came out. On the other hand, having followed him so far he wanted to finish the job. The flats were new and expensive; too expensive for the sort of income earned by a cashier in a firm of estate agents.

A thought occurred to him. He walked across and inspected the lift. The tell-tale above the gate showed that the last person to use it had taken it up to the fourth floor. This was interesting, but not conclusive. If Mr Adams had been making for a flat on the ground floor, or even possibly on the first floor, he might not have used the lift at all.

Milo had a further thought. Each of the flats clearly ran the whole way from the front to the back of the building, one on either side of the central hallway. It was a fair bet that the main living-room would be in front, overlooking the street, with the bedrooms at the back. He turned up the collar of his coat and went out again. The front door of an office building opposite afforded a certain amount of shelter. Milo started to count windows. The top two floors were unlighted. Below that a light showed on the left but not the right. That must be 4a. On the next floor down both sides were black. 2b on the right showed lights, but not 2a.

It was at this point in his observations that Milo realised that he was not alone. Three men were closing in on him, one from either side coming slowly, blocking escape; the third coming straight at him and coming fast.

He had very little time to think. Groping behind he felt for the handle of the door. It was not that he expected it to be open. He wanted something to give him purchase. As the man in the centre launched himself at him he half turned, holding on to the big handle, and kicked. His foot landed low down in the man's stomach. The man gave a sharp gasp, more anger than pain, and folded forward. Milo hurdled his body and made for the doorway of Basildon Mansions. As he reached it, the door opened and a very large woman came out. She was wearing a fur coat and a fur hat, and was attached to a small furry animal. Milo slid past her, kicking the animal as he did so. The woman said, "Really—" and at that moment received the full impact of the first of his pursuers.

By this time Milo was inside the lift and had latched the outer grid. There were two men in the hall. The front one was doing what looked like a slow waltz with a grizzly bear. The second was trying to get past. Milo pressed button number 6. As the inner door slid shut he noted both his opponents making for the stairs.

By the time the lift reached the top floor Milo had done some thinking. Much depended on whether he had put number three out of action. If he had, the simplest plan would be to take the lift down again and bolt for the street. But he rather doubted it. Number three, he guessed, was no worse than winded. If he was now guarding the front hall he could certainly block him until the other two got down. And since it was clear that they knew he could identify them, and were prepared to risk it, this led to a conclusion which was far from comfortable. What he wanted was a place of refuge with a telephone and a more reliable witness than the woman in the fur coat. He had an idea where he might find all three, but it was going to need luck and split-second timing.

He waited, with the inner door of the lift open and the grid shut until the leading pursuer reached the top landing. It was, as he had thought, Len Mason and he guessed that the second one was his brother Chris. Milo was glad to see that both of them had bellows to mind. As they reached the lift he pressed button number 2.

Flat 2b, which had been showing a light, was the flat on the opposite side of the landing. As soon as the lift had stopped, Milo wrenched open the grid, dived across and leaned on the bell.

He could hear the men clattering down the stairs. Also footsteps inside the flat. It was going to be a very close thing.

The door of the flat opened. Milo leaped inside, slammed it behind him and fixed the chain on the door. The occupier of flat 2b was a thin elderly man with silver-grey hair and a placid expression.

He said, "Is somebody chasing you?"

There was a thud on the front door.

Milo said, "I'm afraid that's right, sir."

"Do you think they are going to break down my door?"

"I think they'll try," said Milo. "Have you got a telephone?"

"I have a telephone," said the grey-haired man, "but I fear it is not operative. It has been out of order for a week. The Post Office allege that they are short of staff."

The assault on the door was increasing in fury. The men seemed to have got hold of some sort of battering ram and were smashing it against the wooden panels.

"They'll have the whole door down in a minute," said Milo. "Have you got a back entrance?"

"I have," said the man, "but I have no intention of using it. I intend to defend my domicile."

"I admire your spirit," said Milo, "but these are violent men."

"Then we are entitled to adopt correspondingly violent measures. One moment." He went into the nearest room and reappeared holding a pair of very large old-fashioned pistols.

"I keep them loaded and primed," said the man.

"Have you got a licence for them?"

"Quite unnecessary. They are genuine antiques. See Section 14 of the Firearms Act."

The top part of the door disintegrated and the head

and shoulders of Chris Mason appeared. The grey-haired man said, "I was a magistrate for many years in India and I always held to the view that the law allowed a man to employ a *reasonable* amount of force in countering an unprovoked attack. I am told, by the way, that this weapon throws high."

There was a shattering roar of sound and a jagged hole appeared in the lower panel of the door.

The head and shoulders of Chris Mason disappeared. Sirens sounded at the end of the street.

"That sounds like reinforcements," said Milo. "Let's see if we can get what's left of that door open."

There was a trail of blood on the stairs. When they got down to the hall the Masons and their colleague had disappeared. The open door at the other end of the hall indicated the way they had gone. The fur-coated lady was sitting on the floor with her back to the wall, recovering from a fit of hysterics. The small dog was helping her by washing her face.

"Quite a lot of blood," said the grey-haired man. "Do you think I winged him?"

"More likely splinters from the door panel," said Milo. "If you'd actually hit him with a bullet out of that gun it'd have taken his leg off."

It was the porter who had summoned the police. He now reappeared cautiously from the basement and said, "What's going on here?" The uniformed sergeant from the leading police car said the same thing a moment later. Milo did his best to explain.

"They must have had a car parked somewhere round the back," said Milo. "They got clean away. But I recognised two of them. We could pick them up easily enough."

It was nine o'clock on the following morning. The storm had blown itself out in the night and a pale yellow

sun was lighting, but not warming, the streets of South
London.

"I expect we could," said Petrella coldly. "And all
three of them will deny it and produce convincing alibis
for the whole eveing. I don't imagine Mrs Mapledurham
will be a very convincing witness, and the porter didn't
see them. It'll be your word against theirs."

"I suppose so," said Milo. He was trying to suppress
the father and mother of a sneeze.

"And it won't be very good publicity, will it? A police officer being chivvied up and down stairs by a party
of hooligans. Someone will have to pay for that door,
too."

Milo felt that he was being unfairly treated, but had
been a policeman long enough to know that this happened. Petrella glared round at Blencowe, Ambrose and
Lampier as if daring them to say something. They were
all sensible enough to keep their mouths shut. He said,
"I think it's time we stopped playing cowboys and In-
dians and used our heads. First point, how did they pick
you up so quickly?"

"I suppose Adams spotted me and telephoned for
help."

"Unlikely," said Petrella. "And the timing's much too
quick."

"I'd guess one of them was watching Adams," said
Blencowe. "Just to make certain he wouldn't be followed,
or to take the necessary steps if he was."

"I think so, too," said Petrella. "So that brings us to
the next point. It must have been important to someone
that Adams *wasn't* followed. And I don't believe that
'someone' lives in Basildon Mansions. Adams was using
the front-door-back-door technique. He walked straight
through and out at the back. Leaving you to be attended
to."

"Yesh, arashoo!" said Milo. "Sorry."

"That leads us to a third conclusion," said Petrella. "If they were prepared to go to those lengths to knock you off, it means that the man Mr Adams had come to see must be living fairly close. If he'd been two miles away, Adams would simply have left you standing where you were, catching a cold, and wandered off without bothering about you. I had a look at the area this morning. There are three other blocks of flats. Ashburton Mansions, Chesterfield Court and Devonshire Court. I want a run-down on *all* the people in them. Ambrose and Lampier, you can tackle that. You'll have to do it quietly and tactfully. The best line will be to see if the landlords will help. They must have taken references from their tenants when they moved in. Blencowe, you keep as close to Lloyd as you can. And you,"—he turned round on Milo—"had better go home and put your feet in a mustard bath."

When they were back in their own room Lampier said, "What's eating him? I've never seen him like this before."

"He feels personally involved," said Ambrose. "It's the hot money Lloyd palmed off on him. He's not forgotten that."

Milo said, "Arashoo. I think I'll take him at his word."

It was at ten o'clock that same morning that Mr Adams called at Patton Street Police Station and asked for Petrella. If he knew anything about the events of the night before he showed no signs of it. He perched himself on the chair in front of Petrella's desk, accepted the cigarette that was offered to him and said, "Mr Lloyd sent me along to see if we could interest you in a proposition."

Petrella said, "Yes?"

"You know a lot of people in this district. People

who need flats and other premises from time to time. People who have property to dispose of. If you'd be prepared to keep your ears open and pass these people on to us—you needn't be involved in any other way, except for just mentioning our name—we'd be prepared to pay you a retainer. It's quite a usual arrangement."

"What sort of sum had you in mind?"

"We thought of twenty-five pounds a week. If any business resulted from your introduction there'd be a commission on top of it."

"It's very kind of Mr Lloyd," said Petrella. "But I fear I shall have to say 'no'."

"Think it over."

"I've done all the thinking I'm going to do."

Mr Adams seemed unabashed. He rose to his feet, and turned once more at the door to say, "Think about it."

When he had left, Petrella switched off the tape recorder under his desk. He was smiling, but not agreeably.

Part III

The Peripatetic Birds

The methodical Sergeant Ambrose laid a pile of notes on Petrella's desk and said, "I think we've got them all now, sir. You can read the detailed reports if you like, but in my view there really are only two possibles. Manfred and Samuel Tillotson. They have flats opposite each other, 6a and 6b on the top floor of Chesterfield Court. They're the most expensive flats in the block. They've both got sun terraces. The landlord says they've had the partition between the two terraces removed. That means they have a private access to each other's flats."

"A nice example of brotherly togetherness," said Petrella.

"What do the brothers do when not sunning themselves on adjacent terraces?"

"They have a business in the City. Tillotson (Middle-East) Agencies, Barnaby House, Moorgate. It's in the London telephone directory. All quite open and above-board."

"If so open and above-board, what makes you think they might be villains?"

Ambrose said, "I've seen both of them. They seemed to me—" he was picking his words with care "— to be the only people there of the calibre to be running the sort of show we have in mind."

"In other words," said Petrella, "you're backing instinct. I'm not saying you're wrong. It can be a better horse than science."

On the following morning he took the Underground to the Bank Station and walked down Moorgate. It was nearing the lunch hour and men and girls were pouring out onto the pavements into the mild February sunlight, making the most of their sixty minutes of freedom. Barnaby House was a smallish building on the west side of the road. Petrella spent some time strolling along the opposite pavement, keeping an eye on the door. He noticed three very attractive-looking girls come out together and make off down the street. Then a couple of paunchy middle-aged men, a severe lady in glasses and a group of young men.

When it seemed clear that most of the inhabitants were out of the building he ventured into the hall. A board gave him the information he wanted. Tillotson (Middle-East) Agencies occupied the first floor. The ground floor was Cranmer and Cranmer, Chartered Surveyors and the remaining floors were occupied by Benjamin Dalby and Partners, Solicitors and Commissioners for Oaths.

Petrella made a note of the names and took himself back to the Oval. He found Mr Tasker in his office, lunching off sandwiches and bottled Bass.

"Dalbys," said Mr Tasker, picking his teeth to extract a shred of ham. "Yes. I know them. Nice little firm. Shouldn't have said they'd touch anything crooked."

"I wasn't thinking of them as being crooked. It's their neighbours I'm interested in. Do you happen to know any of the partners?"

Mr Tasker consulted the Law List and said, "As a matter of fact I do. Young Buckle used to be an articled clerk here. Lazy young devil. I could give him a ring. Have to tell him some sort of story."

"Tell him the truth. Say I'm interested in one of the parties who uses the building."

Mr Tasker looked at his watch. He said, "We won't catch him at the office now. Never took less than two hours for his lunch when he was articled here. Probably takes three now he's a partner. I'll ring him this afternoon. There are plenty of good pubs in the City. Offer him lunch at one of them tomorrow."

Young Mr Buckle turned out to be an entertaining lunch companion. He said several disrespectful things about Mr Tasker, but obviously admired him. When Petrella brought the conversation round to Tillotsons, Mr Buckle said, "As soon as I heard you were interested in someone in the building I guessed it must be them. They're a mystery outfit, they really are."

"In what way?"

"Well, they've got an expensive set of offices and a super line in staff, but they never seem to have any customers. And what's more—you can't help noticing these things when you work in the same building—they never seem to get any mail."

"Maybe they do all their work by telephone and telex."

"It's possible. But in that case, what do you suppose those lovelies do all day? Sit on their boss's knee?"

"Would they be the three girls I saw coming out of the place yesterday?"

"If they were worth a second look, they must have been. Cranmers seem to go in for an all-male staff and we haven't got a female in the place under forty, the idea being to keep our minds on our work, I imagine."

"Those three were certainly worth looking at," agreed Petrella.

"And I'll tell you another odd thing about them. They go away and come back again. Did you notice one of them, a brunette with a snub nose and a page-boy haircut?"

"Yes. She was the one in the middle. What about her?"

"She disappeared just after Christmas. Not this Christmas, the one before. Then she came back, sometime in May, and the red-head took off. She was back in October."

Petrella listened, fascinated. He said, "Is anyone missing now?"

"I'll say. It's the blonde. Pick of the bunch. Shoulder-length hair and green eyes. She went off about the time the red-head came back."

"You seem to keep a close eye on their comings and goings."

Young Mr Buckle said, without a blush on his downy cheeks, "I'm a devoted bird watcher."

Petrella returned thoughtfully to Patton Street. He felt certain that he had his hand on one of the threads, one of the clues to the labyrinth, but he could not yet disentangle it. Why should two business men keep three or four attractive and presumably expensive girls in an office, doing nothing all day. Unless, of course, they had insatiable sexual appetites, but then, surely, it would be cheaper, rents in the City being what they were, to have installed them in flats. Maybe they had got a perfectly genuine tie-up with the Middle East. There was plenty of money there and a smashing girl would be a useful maker of contacts. But somehow he doubted it. Like Sergeant Ambrose, he was guided in such matters more by instinct than by reasoning.

He said to Lampier, "You've got one of those candid-camera arrangements. I want you to photograph three young ladies. You can probably get them all in one shot as they come out for lunch. Only for God's sake don't be caught doing it. Then have the three faces screened and enlarged."

A few evenings later Samuel strolled across to talk to Manfred. He found his brother listening to the long-range weather forecast. He said, "It seems that we are to have more than the average amount of rain this month. Some high winds to start with, dying down later, with possibilities of fog. No ice."

"It sounds just what the doctor ordered," said Samuel. "A few fog patches on the fourteenth, but no ice on the road. It will suit us down to the ground."

"Eight days to go."

Samuel said, "I saw an advertisement in the Sunday papers. I've been making some enquiries about it. A villa in the hills to the east of Beirut. Twenty thousand pounds sterling, or the equivalent in local currency."

"Are you thinking of buying it?"

"I've made an offer."

"I see," said Manfred. "So you have decided it is time we retired?"

"Our local contacts could organise the transfer of our funds. We should lose fifteen per cent on the transaction, but it would be worth it."

"Is something worrying you?"

"A lot of little things. There seem to have been one or two people, with nothing to do, on the pavement outside Barnaby House lately. It could be my imagination."

"And?"

Samuel said slowly, "I am not happy about Julie."

"You needn't worry about her. I have traced her family. It wasn't difficult. They live in the Liverpool suburb of Litherland. Until Julie came to London she had spent all her life there. The envelope was obviously planted for Ma Dalby. But she's not a police spy."

"A greedy little girl who knows too much could be more dangerous than a police spy," said Samuel. "Remember also, she has never actually done a job for us yet. That leaves her free to talk if she wants to."

"What are you suggesting?" said Manfred. He was beginning to sound angry.

"Nothing drastic. I suggest we get the boys to throw a scare into her. Enough to keep her quiet until after the fourteenth. That's all."

Manfred thought about it. He said, "I agree that we don't want to take any chances at this particular time. But if you do what you suggest, I think you will be making trouble where none existed before."

"Let's sleep on it," said Samuel. He looked at his watch. "Adams should be ringing."

"He's usually very punctual," said Manfred. "Have a drink." He was half-way to the drink table when the telephone rang. He picked up the receiver, and conducted a one-sided conversation which consisted chiefly of grunts on his part. Finally he said, "I'll pick you up in my car at the road junction in the middle of Blackheath at seven o'clock tomorrow."

His brother said, "Has there been some development?"

"Yes and no. I asked Adams to find out if there was any particular reason why he should have been followed the other night. He thinks he has found the reason. I am going to discuss it with him. If he is right, we may have to think very carefully about it."

"I leave the thinking to you," said Samuel, "with every confidence." He put an arm round his brother's broad shoulders and gave him an affectionate squeeze.

Petrella sat up in bed and said, "Of course."

"Of course what?" said his wife sleepily.

"It must be the answer."

"Go to sleep," said his wife.

Ideas which arrive at two o'clock in the morning sometimes turn out to be chimeras, but at breakfast time the idea still looked solid. As soon as he got to Patton Street he sent for Sergeant Ambrose. He said, "Go round to these three addresses, see the managing director first and then get hold of the chap who's in charge of hirings and firings."

"The personnel manager."

"Right."

"And what do I ask him?"

"I've written down two dates opposite each name. I want to know if a girl was taken on around the first date and quit around the second."

"They're all fairly large outfits."

"Certainly. But I'm not talking about a girl in the factory. I mean someone who had a job in the executive office. Secretary or P.A. to one of the top bods. Something like that."

"And if they say yes?"

"Show them the photographs."

The long-range weather forecast had got away to an accurate start. A cold, heavy rain was coming straight down out of a black sky. Mr Adams turned up the collar of his coat and cursed Manfred Tillotson for choosing such a desolate spot for his rendezvous.

A Vauxhall Magnum drew up to the kerb. Manfred said, "Get in. Take your coat off and throw it on to the back seat."

The car heater was on and the interior was warm and comfortable. Manfred said, "There's a flask in the pocket beside you. Help yourself." They drove on for a few minutes in silence. They seemed to be making their way down off the heath, towards the river.

At the bottom of Maze Hill Manfred swung the car into a side turning, drew up, and said, "Well, what's the answer?"

"I'm afraid Mr Lloyd's getting careless."

"In what way?"

"When he paid one of our customers in cash he gave him thirty of the new tenners from the Corinth job."

"Thirty?" said Manfred thoughtfully. "He might have thinned them out a bit more than that. Still, it's all part of the system isn't it?"

"It wasn't the number of notes, it was the person he gave them to. Chief Inspector Petrella."

"He did *what*?"

"That's right. Petrella's our local gaffer at Patton Street."

There was a long silence whilst Manfred thought this over. Then he said, "We all know the Yard keeps an eye on senior officers' accounts. That must be how they spotted it." He was silent again, thinking out the ramifications of this new development. It had been worrying when he had not known why Adams had been followed. Now that he had the explanation it was less alarming. But there was a possibility that had to be checked.

"Is there any chance," he said, "that Lloyd did it on purpose?"

Mr Adams turned his head. The car had been carefully parked half-way between lamp posts. There was not enough light for him to see Manfred's face clearly. He said, "I *think* it was just a slip up."

"But you're not sure. Why?"

"He's been seeing a lot of one of the sergeants from Patton Street. A Welshman called Blencowe. They talk rugby football."

"All the time?" said Manfred. "Or just when anyone else is listening."

"It's in the Wheelwrights. They have a couple of beers there most evenings. I didn't think—"

"That's right," said Manfred. "You didn't think."

But he was thinking, turning over possibilities, making plans against a contingency which ought to have been foreseen and now had to be dealt with. He was silent for so long that, in the end, it was Mr Adams who spoke. He said, "The fact is, he's getting old. And tired. I don't think he means to tell them anything, but if they keep hammering at him, he might fall apart."

"Don't upset yourself about it," said Manfred. "It's not your problem. I'll drop you at your flat."

When Julie left Chesterfield Court at about seven o'clock, two evenings later, she had in her handbag a letter from her mother. It had reached her by a round-about route, through the good offices of a friend of a friend. Mrs Marsh was not a great letter-writer. The four pages were punctuated with exclamation marks and scored with underlining, but their message could have been put in two words, "Come home".

Julie considered the proposition coolly. There had been moments, in the last week, when she had sensed undercurrents of distrust in the curious little circle into which she had fallen. Nobody had said anything. Possibly what had worried her were things which would have been said before and weren't being said now. On the other hand, the conditions were easy and the pay was fabulous. She had a sudden picture of home. The streets of Litherland. Men and girls trooping off at eight o'clock on a grey morning to a day's work and trooping back again in the evening tired, but planning a night out at the local with a crowd of boys; boys with unsuccessful moustaches; boys who smelled of beer and cigarettes and talked about nothing but soccer. It was familiar and it was safe; but my God, it was dull.

She was still thinking about this when she got off the train at Borough Station and started to walk home to her topfloor flat in Manciple Street. She was half-way there when the car drew up just ahead of her and a man got out. She had seem him twice before with Manfred, but didn't know his name. He said, "Hop in chick, we'll take you home."

"Not worth it," said Julie. "It's only two streets on."

"Come on."

"What do you think my legs are for?"

"I could give you one or two answers to that," said Mason coming closer. "But don't let's stop here all night discussing it. Just get in."

"I told you, no."

Mason came so close to her that she had to step back. She found herself up against railings. Mason said, lowering his face towards her, "In my book, little girls do what they're told. If they don't, they're apt to lose things. Like, say, bits of their face."

She saw the bright gleam of steel in his right hand, held down by his side. She also saw that a man was coming along the pavement towards her.

She screamed out, "Leave me alone."

The newcomer rolled to a halt. He was as big as Mason and was smiling in a good-natured way. He said, "Phwat goes on here?" The lilt in his voice proclaimed an Irishman.

"I should advise you to keep walking, chum," said Mason.

"Would you now," said the newcomer. "And suppose I were to ask the little lady if she was in trouble."

"He's trying to get me into that car," said Julie.

"If you don't care to go with him," said the newcomer judicially, "then there's no reason you should. No reason at all."

By this time the driver had got out of the car. Mason said, "For the last time, if you don't keep your fucking nose out of our business, you'll get fucking-well hurt."

The newcomer gave a long whistle, apparently of surprise. He said, "Hey, Patrick. Would you believe it. I'm being intimidated."

A second man appeared on the scene. He said, "Whadder you know?" He had approached very quietly. Mason could see a third figure in the shadows behind him. He sensed that there might be others. He was outside his own territory. It was no moment for taking chances. He swung round, signalled to the driver and climbed back into the car.

The three men on the pavement watched in silence as the car drove off. The first one said, "We could use that taxi of yours, Len."

"It's just round the corner. I'll fetch it."

"You do that. The little lady's had a bad fright. I can see that."

"It's very good of you," said Julie faintly. Her legs seemed to be in danger of giving way under her.

"Think nothing of it," said the first man. "It's a sad world if we can't spread a little light and happiness. You go with Len. He'll take you home right enough."

Julie said, "It's only three streets away. It's hardly worth bothering." But she got in.

"You come from Liverpool, I guess," said Len. "There's a coincidence, for it's my own home town."

As they drove off, Julie was coming to a decision. All her money and her important possessions were in her handbag. There was nothing in her flat that she couldn't replace. She opened the glass partition and said, "I've changed my mind. Do you think you could drive me to Euston?"

Len seemed unsurprised. He executed a tight U-turn and set off in the opposite direction. When they got to Euston his kindness was not exhausted. He parked the taxi against the kerb, put a glove over the meter and said, "I'll come along with you whilst you find your train. That is, if you've no objection."

He was a square, solid comforting sort of person. Julie smiled at him and said, "I'd like that, Len. Are you sure you won't get into trouble leaving your cab there?"

"No trouble I can't get out of," said Len.

They found that an Inter-City train was leaving for Liverpool in ten minutes, which gave them time to buy her a ticket and some newspapers to read.

Len waved to her in a fatherly way as the train drew out. Then he moved off to the nearest telephone box—

"Get round to her place, then, and wait for her," said Manfred.

"We did that," said Mason. "We waited more than an hour. She never turned up. I think she's scarpered."

"Scarpered where?"

"Back home to Liverpool would be my guess."

"Did you hurt her?"

"We didn't touch her. Never had a chance. This other lot turned up. Paddies. Four or five of 'em."

Samuel, who had been listening on an extension line said, "What makes you think she's gone back to Liverpool?"

"She'd been talking about it to the other girls. I think she had a letter from her mum."

"One of you had better watch her flat. Take it in turns. If she shows up, report back. But no further action until we tell you."

When he had put down the receiver he said, "I don't like it."

"What's wrong with it?" said Manfred. "We told the boys to throw a scare into her and they've done it. Not quite the way we intended, I agree. But if she really has gone home to mum, that's what we wanted, isn't it?"

"*If* she keeps her mouth shut."

"She knows what'll happen to her if she doesn't."

"Maybe," said Samuel. "I still don't like it. It happened too conveniently. Those men being on the spot."

"There are a lot of Irishmen in that area. They work in the leather market and the goods depot at Bricklayers Arms."

"I know," said Samuel. "I know."

Manfred looked at him curiously. He had a respect for his brother's instinct, but on this occasion he seemed to be stretching it. He said, "We know Julie's address and we've got friends in Liverpool. Why don't we ask one of them to go out to her house tomorrow? He'll find out soon enough if she's there."

By the time the eight-twenty Inter-City train from Euston reached Lime Street Station, Liverpool, Julie was three parts asleep. She stumbled out on to the platform and wandered down it, trailing behind the other passengers. She was trying to work out exactly what she was going to say to her mother and how she was going to explain her arrival in the middle of the night equipped only with the contents of one large handbag.

It was some seconds before she realised that the man with grey hair was speaking to her. He said, "You are Miss Marsh, aren't you? I'm Detective Inspector Lander. This is my warrant card. Oh, and the policeman in the booking hall will identify me, if that'll make you happier. A lot of people don't know what a warrant card looks like anyway."

"I'll believe you," said Julie. "What do you want?"

"We thought it might be useful if you'd agree to come along to the Station and make a short statement. After that we could run you home. You won't find it too easy to get a taxi to take you out to Litherland at this time of night."

It took Julie only five seconds to make up her mind.

It was at about six o'clock on the following evening that Sergeant Milo Roughead said to Petrella, "I think I've got it, sir."

"Measles, the D.S.O., or a ticket to the Police Federation Ball?"

"None of those," said Milo. He was relieved to note that Petrella's customary good humour seemed to have returned. "It's an idea."

"I'll buy it. But it had better be good."

"This idea is absolutely top line. Do you think that Lloyd and Lloyd might have been set up as cleaners?"

"Come again."

"It's an idea the Mafia developed in America. They get hold of a lot of hot money through narcotics and prostitution and gambling and things like that. But they also control a few absolutely straight businesses as well. Places that keep books and have bank accounts. They feed the dirty cash into them and it comes out the other end on a nice clean respectable bank statement."

Petrella thought about it. He said, "How exactly would it work in this case?"

"If the people at the top are in the wage-snatch game they must be lumbered with a lot of banknotes. Not always new, like those tenners they passed off on you. Usually old small-denomination stuff. All the same, they can't just turn up at a bank with a sackful of them and say, 'Credit this to my private account'. Not without a few questions being asked. So they pass it on to Lloyd and Lloyd. They do most of their buying for cash. That means the stuff gets well spread out. When they sell, they take a cheque in the ordinary way and pay it into their bank. How to wash your money whiter than white in two simple processes."

"Then you think Lloyd's in it himself?"

"I think he must be, sir. And another person who'd have to be in the know was the chap who did the legal work of buying and selling. If he wasn't in the game he'd be bound to ask why all the purchases were for cash and the sales were paid for by cheque."

"Bernie Nicholls," said Petrella. In the march of events during the last six weeks he had almost forgotten that body, face downwards on the frozen foreshore of the river.

"What about Adams?"

"I should think he was put in by the Tillotsons to keep an eye on Lloyd. I don't mean that they actually distrusted Lloyd. But it must have been handy to have their own creature in the organisation too. He'd be under their thumb, because they knew about his record."

The more Petrella thought about it, the more sense it made. He said, "I'm not sure how we're ever going to prove it, but I think you're right."

"Can we tie the Tillotsons to it?"

"We can tie the Tillotsons to the wage snatches all right," said Petrella. "We can tie them with three sweet little clove hitches. Their names are Sandra, Avril and Jayne. They all work, or pretend to work, for Tillotsons (Middle-East) Agencies. Let us suppose that you are the personnel manager of Corinth Car Parts. You need a secretary to work in the accounts department. You advertise. Past experience has shown you that you won't get many applicants and will probably have to fall back on paying an exorbitant fee to an employment agency. However, to your surprise and delight an applicant turns up who has every qualification, is prepared to accept the wage you offer without quibbling, and, as an extra which must appeal to a susceptible personnel manager, happens to be a very attractive-looking girl. What do you do?"

"I hold my breath," said Milo, "and ask for a reference from her last employer."

"Her last employer is Tillotsons (Middle-East) Agencies. They give her a glowing reference. They are very sorry to lose her. She is only leaving them because she finds the journey to work difficult."

"And did this actually happen?"

"It happened three times. Sandra, who is a blonde with shoulder-length hair and green eyes, joined Corinth Car Parts in the autumn of the year before last. They lost a large wage packet in early November of that year. She was back at Tillotsons by Christmas time. At about that date Avril, a brunette with a snub nose and a page-boy cut—you'll find her photograph, it's numbered 1, in that folder—"

Milo examined the photograph with appreciation. He said, "Let me guess. She joined G.E.X. and left them shortly after their wage snatch in April."

"Absolutely correct. And Jayne—she's the red-head— No. 2 photograph, joined Costa-Cans in May, and was back in the nest by October."

"Who's Number 3?"

"Her name is Julie and she comes from Liverpool. I think she must be on probation. As far as I know they haven't loosed her on British industry yet. They must be saving her up for the next job."

Milo was examining the three photographs. He said, "Those are the three girls who are currently at Tillotsons, I take it."

"Correct. Lampier photographed them as they were coming out to lunch last week."

"Then where is Sandra?"

"If we knew that," said Petrella, "we should know where the *next* big wage snatch was going to take place." On these words Petrella's desk telephone gave a buzz and Station Sergeant Cove said, "I thought you might like to know, Superintendent Watterson's on his way up. He's got the top brass with him."

Petrella said, "Thanks, Harry." And to Milo, "I don't suppose they've come to give us a Valentine. You'd better clear out."

Commander Baylis came straight to the point. He said, "The general manager of G.E.X. Engineering put in a report that one of your men had been round at his place asking questions. He wanted to know what it was all about. So do I."

Petrella said, "You might have had similar reports

from Corinth Car Parts and Costa-Cans, sir. Sergeant Ambrose visited all three."

"Would you mind explaining why?"

Petrella did his best.

"And who authorised you to investigate these three wage snatches?"

Petrella said, "I wasn't investigating the wage snatches. I was investigating two men called Tillotson. I arrived at them in the course of an enquiry into the affairs of Lloyd and Lloyd, which was authorised by you personally."

Watterson said, "You remember, sir. This arose indirectly out of the death—suspected murder—of a man called Nicholls."

"Precisely," said Baylis. He said it in the pleased tone of a small man about to score a small point. "Correct me if I'm wrong, Superintendent; but I understood that the body in question was not found in this Station area at all."

"You're right," said Watterson. "By a matter of a hundred yards. It belonged to Loveday, at Borough."

"Then will you please hand it back to him."

Petrella was now as angry as Baylis. Disregarding a warning look from Watterson he said, "Since Lloyd and Lloyd *are* in my area I assume I'm allowed to continue my investigation into their affairs."

"Then you assume wrongly. To the best of my knowledge, and I have had quite a lot to do with them, Lloyd and Lloyd are a perfectly respectable firm. It is not my job to allocate your duties, but if I was in Watterson's place I'd instruct you to attend to more serious matters—confining your attention to your own Station area."

He stalked out, leaving Petrella and Watterson staring at each other.

"What on earth's biting him?" said Petrella.

Watterson blew his nose in the peculiar trumpeting manner which Petrella recognised as meaning that he wanted time to think. He said, "If it was just the wage snatches, Patrick, I could understand that. They're S.C.S. jobs and he's not even allowed to touch them himself. So you can imagine he wouldn't be too pleased at you butting in. But warning you off Lloyd and Lloyd just doesn't make sense."

Sergeant Blencowe put his head round the door and said, "Sorry to interrupt, but I thought you ought to have this at once. Owers just found Mr Lloyd in an alley off the Cut. Head smashed in. Whoever did it dragged the body into a doorway and covered it with sacks. Owers spotted his boots."

"Well now," said Watterson. "That's different. It's in your area, isn't it?"

"It certainly is."

"Then I don't see how anyone can object if we investigate this one, do you?"

Part IV

St Valentine's Day

St Valentine's Day was cold, but bright.

By nine o'clock Petrella was at the Kentledge Road Mortuary. The Coroner's officer took him through the public offices, into the long back room with overhead fluorescent lighting where the body of Jimmy Lloyd, stripped of all clothes and all human dignity, lay on a slab.

Dr Summerson came out of a room at the back wearing a white surgical gown and pulling on a pair of thin rubber gloves.

He said, "Good morning, Patrick. 'Q' Division are keeping us busy these days." And to the mortuary assistant, "Hand me those scissors, would you, Fred. I'd like to get some of the hair away. Then we can take a proper look at the damage."

Petrella watched him at work, snipping away the dank grey strands of hair and swabbing off the blackened blood. He had watched too many post-mortems to be badly upset, but it usually took a minute or two for his stomach to settle.

"Not much external bleeding. A very deep impacted fracture, about an inch to the right of the centre of the rear occipital dome. Did you get that, Lucy?"

Petrella realised that he was speaking to his secretary who was in the back room taking notes. She said, "How many 'c's'."

"Two for preference," said Dr Summerson. "Wonderful girl, but can't spell her own name. I am removing a number of splinters of bone and will place them separately in an envelope marked L/A. I can now see into the wound which seems to me—" a pause for probing, "— to be just over two inches deep at its point of greatest penetration. Would you care to have a look at it, Patrick?"

Petrella peered cautiously into the cavity. He presumed that the grey matter at the bottom of it was brain tissue. He said, "What do you suppose did it?"

"It wasn't anything very sharp. Nothing like an ice pick, for instance. More like the blunt end of a hammer. Judging from the point of impact and the direction of the blow the man who hit him was several inches taller than Lloyd, right handed and standing almost directly behind him. We may know a bit more when the laboratory has finished with these bone fragments. They'll pick up traces of rust, things like that."

When Petrella came out, the Coroner's officer had the contents of Mr Lloyd's pockets arranged on the table. A packet of Senior Service cigarettes and a Ronson lighter.

Three felt-tipped pens, one black, one red and one green. A cheque book. A fat black wallet with a rubber band round it. Two dirty handkerchiefs, a bunch of keys and a pile of loose coins. In the wallet, fifteen pounds in notes, a number of different credit cards, two uncashed cheques for small amounts, a new book of stamps, with one stamp missing and a photograph of two small girls with the words, "For Grandfather" written on the back.

"Better list them and let me have a copy," said Petrella. There was an odd-looking coin among the loose change. When he picked it up he saw that it was a polished metal disc with a hole in the middle.

"Shove ha'penny," said the Coroner's officer. "Poor old Jimmy. He must have been pretty pissed if he put that in his pocket in mistake for a tenpenny piece."

"I'd better give it back to its owner," said Petrella. His next call was at the Wheelwrights Arms where he was let in by the side door. Mr Elder identified the metal disc as his property and said, "Poor old Jimmy. I wouldn't have been surprised if he'd walked off with the dartboard actually."

"Was he as drunk as all that?"

"He wasn't drunk. He was just—I don't know—he wasn't with it at all."

"What exactly do you mean?"

"Well—he came in about eight o'clock and asked for a double Scotch, and took it over to a table in the corner, and put it down and seemed to forget about it."

"You mean he just sat there?"

"That's right. Until Charlie Cousins went over to talk to him. Then he seemed to remember it was there and drank it off quickly. Charlie came back to the bar for another round and said, 'What's up with old Lloyd? He isn't making much sense at all.' However, as I said, he wasn't drunk. One or two other people went across to chat him up and they got him playing on the shove ha'penny board. He seemed to be going a bit better at that point. Then, quite suddenly, right in the middle of a game, he said, 'I'm sorry, lads. This isn't my night,' and walked straight out."

"What time would that have been?"

"About half past ten."

"Did you get any idea what was wrong with him?"

"Not from anything he said. It did put me in mind of Jimmy Wilson. You wouldn't remember him. It was before your time. He came in here one evening and behaved just like that. Walked out at closing time and threw himself off Tower Bridge. Of course, we only found out afterwards his wife had been killed in a car smash that afternoon."

The telephone at the back of the bar rang. Mr Elder lifted off the receiver, listened for a moment and said, "It's for you."

It was Sergeant Blencowe. He said, "I'm round at Lloyd's office. The girls are in a bit of a flap. Adams hasn't put in an appearance."

Petrella said, "I'll be right over."

When he got there he found the two girls in the outer office twittering with the pleasurable sort of excitement which is produced by a crisis for which you have no sort of responsibility. In the inner room Sergeant Blencowe was talking to the sad solicitor, Mr Lampe. Mr Lampe said, "I heard the shocking news about James Lloyd and I came straight round. I really don't know what to do. Since Nicholls died I've been handling Lloyd's business myself. There were half a dozen outstanding matters which had to be cleared up. My conveyancing is a bit rusty, but luckily they were none of them too complicated. Straight sales and purchases.

One of them was due to be completed this morning. The purchase of the stock of a sweet shop and tobacconist."

"For cash?" said Petrella.

"Why, yes. It was for cash. Most of Mr Lloyd's purchases seem to have been made that way. I confess I thought it rather curious."

"And you were coming round here to collect the money from Mr Lloyd."

"Mr Adams usually dealt with matters like that."

"I see," said Petrella. It was confirmation. "I suppose the cash was kept in some sort of safe."

"It's next door," said Blencowe. "And some sort of safe is right." They all went into the adjoining room. The green and gold monster was set solidly into the brickwork of what had once been a fireplace.

"You wouldn't open that with a bent hairpin," said Blencowe.

"Who's got the keys?"

"I asked the girls," said Blencowe. "Old man Lloyd had one set. Adams had the other."

"Nip down to the mortuary," said Petrella. "There was a bunch of keys on Lloyd. I'll give them a ring from here and tell them you're coming."

Blencowe was back in ten minutes. There was only one key that looked like a safe key. Petrella slid it into the lock with an odd feeling of anticipation. It turned smoothly. He pulled down the handle and swung the heavy door open.

There were three shelves which held a few bundles of deeds and leases, carefully tied in red tape. The space under the bottom shelf was occupied by a locked steel drawer.

"That's where the cash was always kept," said Mr Lampe, who was peering over his shoulder. Petrella found the right key pulled open the drawer. It was empty.

He said to Mr Lampe, "You were coming round here, you told us, to collect the cash to complete this purchase. How much was it?"

"Nine hundred pounds."

"And you've had cash from here before."

"Oh yes. Several times. Once nearly two thousand pounds. I told Mr Lloyd that it was foolish to keep it all here, even in a modern safe like this. The insurance companies are apt to make trouble about that sort of thing."

"How much do you suppose he had here at a time?"

"It's difficult to say. I remember Nicholls telling me that he once paid out five thousand pounds in five-pound notes."

"The cupboard's bare now," said Blencowe.

Petrella said, "Take a car and go straight out to Blackheath. You know Adams's address. If he's there, invite him to come back with you to the Station. If he won't come, telephone me. But don't let him out of your sight."

"And if he isn't there?" said Blencowe.

"I'd like to know that, as soon as possible."

There was something else at the back of his mind. It was connected with the bunch of keys. Something which might be important. It was no good trying to force it. Either he would think of it, or he wouldn't.

Manfred looked at his watch, and said, "Five past eleven. He isn't often late on a time call."

"He may have been held up," said Samuel. "Any news of that girl?"

"Nothing but good news. She hasn't been out of the house this morning."

"She might have been talking on the telephone."

"She might have been," said Manfred. "*If* the house

was on the phone, which it isn't. I told you you were worrying about nothing."

"I don't worry about nothing," said Samuel. "What I worry about is things I can't understand."

"Such as—?"

"Such as what happened yesterday evening. I had a word with young Mason. He was driving the car and he got out to help his brother. He was a bit more honest than Chris. It wasn't five or six Paddies. It was just three of them."

"Three?"

"That's what he said."

"And they walked away from them. Why?"

"What he said was, he thought his brother was right to pull out. He said, suppose we'd started something, and the police had turned up and we'd all been pulled in, who was going to handle the job today?"

"Justifiable."

"Justifiable," agreed Samuel. "But quite untypical. Those boys hit first and think afterwards."

"You've got some idea in your head about it," said Manfred patiently. "Let's have it."

"People like the Masons, who live by violence, get a sort of instinct about the opposition. Either it's amateur or it's professional. If it's amateur, they go in happily and knock hell out of it. If it's professional, they think twice."

Manfred was about to say something when the telephone rang. He said, "That'll be Adams. And about time too."

It wasn't Adams. A woman's voice said, "Is that the Water Board?"

"I'm afraid you have the wrong number," said Manfred.

The woman was still apologising when he rang off.

"He's gone," said Blencowe. "Packed up late last night and pulled out. It's one of those old houses, carved up into flats. The sort of place where everyone knows what everyone else is doing. The old codger on the second floor says he heard him arrive about eleven o'clock, by taxi. What really interested him was that Adams kept the taxi waiting. For about half an hour, he says, whilst he banged about upstairs. Then he came out, with a suitcase in either hand, climbed into the taxi and drove off. The lady on the first floor heard him, too. He woke her child up when he slammed the front door. She was very cross about it."

"I don't suppose, by any chance," said Petrella, "that anyone heard where he told the taxi to go to."

"Certainly they did. They all had their windows open by that time. He told him to go to Victoria."

Petrella said, "I think we've got enough to put out an all Stations call."

"Could be out of the country by now."

"I don't think so," said Petrella. "He wouldn't find a boat train at that time of night. I think Victoria was bluff. He's gone to earth somewhere."

He rang through to Division, found Watterson here, and explained what had happened. Watterson listened carefully and then said, "If that solicitor is prepared to say that there was normally a very substantial amount of cash kept in that safe, of which Adams had the only other key, and if he's disappeared and the safe's empty, we should be able to justify a general call. They have to alert the various exit points as well. It's quite an elaborate operation. I'll get the wheels turning."

Petrella put down the telephone and started to work out timings. Adams had decided to quit, no doubt, because he saw himself going the same way as Bernie Nicholls and old Mr Lloyd. He had grabbed whatever money was in the safe and left his flat. So far, so good. But what had happened next?

There was no train with a cross-Channel connection after ten o'clock at night. On the other hand, there were night flights from Heathrow. If Adams had made his preparations in advance—and he was the careful sort of man who might well have done so—he could by now be almost anywhere in the world.

It was at this point in his reflections that Petrella's subconscious got through to him with its message. It might have been some vague connection between "all the countries in the world" and a stamp album he had possessed in his youth, or it might have been simple coincidence. A new stamp book, with one stamp missing. He said to Blencowe, "What time did you leave your flat this morning?"

"Eight o'clock," said Blencowe.

"Had the post come?"

"Doesn't arrive till half past eight earliest."

"Telephone your wife and ask if there's a letter for you."

Blencowe looked surprised, but went out to his own room. He was back in a few minutes and said, "Bang on the nail, Skipper. Local postmark. Timed seven o'clock last night. What's in it—a bomb?"

"Something of the sort," said Petrella. "Get hold of it quickly. Take the car."

They were finishing reading the letter when Watterson arrived. They showed it to him and he read it in silence. It was two sheets of Mr Lloyd's office paper covered on both sides with Mr Lloyd's cramped handwriting and it contained a full and exact description of the money cleaning activities which he and Adams had been carrying out for the Tillotsons during the past five years. Names, dates, the lot.

Watterson was silent when he had finished reading. Something seemed to be worrying him. Petrella said, "When he wrote that he knew he was for it. And he just bloody well didn't care." There was a further moment of silence. Petrella said, "I hope they catch Adams before he gets out of the country."

Watterson said, "I had to put your request for an all stations alert through District. They turned it down."

Petrella felt himself going red. He said, "Baylis turned it down? What the hell's he playing at?"

Watterson looked at Blencowe, who removed himself quietly from the room. Then he said, "That's right. Baylis turned it down personally. Half an hour ago. That's what I came to tell you."

"He realised that Adams was most probably leaving the country?"

"He had all the relevant information."

"And he doesn't want him stopped?"

Watterson didn't answer this immediately. He had known Petrella for a long time, and had worked directly with him for nearly a year. He knew him to be a cool and controlled person, persistent where persistence was needed, but not stupidly obstinate. A man who would be guided, ninety-nine times out of a hundred, by reason and not by passion.

But he also knew that Petrella's father was Spanish, being high up in the Spanish Intelligence Service; and that there was, deep down inside Petrella, normally kept under lock and key, a black Iberian demon. He himself had seen it in action only once. It was a sight he had not forgotten.

Since Petrella seemed to be waiting for an answer to his last question he said, "All I can tell you is that District refused to sanction your request for a general alert and a port watch. And that the refusal came personally from Commander Baylis."

"No reason given."

"Not to me."

Petrella said, "I see." His voice was controlled again, but it was the control of a fury which was now cold rather than hot. He thought for a moment, and then said, "A short time ago. Adams came into this room and offered me a bribe. It was a large bribe and well wrapped up. He said that if I kept my eyes and ears open for possible clients for Lloyd and Lloyd he would pay me twenty-five pounds a week, with commission on top. He seemed surprised when I turned it down. What he didn't know was that the whole conversation was taped. You can hear it if you like."

"I'll take your word for it. What does it lead to?"

"It leads me to wonder how much he was paying Commander Baylis."

Watterson said, without any inflection of either surprise or anger in his voice, "The fact that Adams tried to bribe you doesn't prove that he succeeded in bribing Baylis."

"It doesn't prove it," said Petrella. "But consider the facts. First, he's got a very expensive wife. You told me so yourself. Second, he personally blocked any further investigation into the affairs of Lloyd and Lloyd. A very respectable firm he called them; you remember?"

"Did you tape that conversation as well?"

"No. But you heard it. And wouldn't, I imagine, deny it."

"Go on."

"Finally he's stopped us taking the most obvious and elementary steps to catch Adams. Why? There can only be one reason. He doesn't want him caught. Because if he's caught, he'll talk. And now that Lloyd's dead, Adams is the only person who can incriminate Baylis."

There was a long silence, in which they heard a car in the street outside run into another car and a furious row start up. Neither man so much as glanced at the window.

At last, Watterson gave a sigh which seemed to let a lot of air out of his lungs. Then he said, "What do you propose to do about it?"

"There's only one thing we can do. We shall have to go over his head."

"When you say 'we' are you proposing that I should support you?"

"I don't need your support. I only ask you to forward my request."

"You realise that you're putting your own head on the block. Unless you can prove what you're saying, prove it to the hilt, you're finished in the police."

"I don't think," said Petrella coldly, "that I should care to remain a member of a force that could let Baylis get away with this sort of thing."

"Always supposing that you're right."

"I'm right," said Petrella. "And you know that I'm right."

"What makes you think that?"

"If you hadn't known I was right, you'd have started shouting the odds long ago."

Watterson managed a faint smile. He said, "An application to see the top brass normally takes time. But it can be expedited. I'll see what I can do."

Petrella walked from Waterloo Station, down York Road, through the deserted forecourt of County Hall and over Westminster Bridge. He found the action of walking useful when he wanted to think.

A message had come through at midday. It simply said that the Assistant Commissioner would see him at ten minutes to three that afternoon. Petrella had spent most of the interval putting the case against Commander Baylis into logical order. In the form of notes, it now covered two sheets of foolscap, neatly folded and slipped into the breast pocket of his coat. He was under no illusions as to what lay ahead. The man he was going to deal with had been a barrister before he became a policeman. He had a coldly logical brain and a tongue which was feared from one end of the Metropolitan Police to the other.

This was the reason for the notes. Not that Petrella had any intention of producing them and reading from them. He had learned them by heart. They were in his pocket as a form of talisman.

As he reached Parliament Square, Big Ben showed twenty minutes to three.

The Tillotsons sat together in Manfred's drawing-room. It was five minutes since either of them had opened his mouth. Then Manfred said, "You're still worried about something. Is it that girl?"

"Julie?" said Samuel. "No. I don't think she can do us any harm now. I was wondering about Adams."

"If he knows what's good for him," said Manfred, "he'll be out of the country."

Silence fell again. Samuel looked at his watch and said, "They should be going in now. We'll hear, one way or another, inside fifteen minutes."

A moment later, when the bell rang, he instinctively put his hand out for the telephone. Then he realised that it was the door bell.

"Were we expecting visitors?" said Manfred.

"Not to my knowledge," said Samuel. "I'd better go and see who it is."

His brother said, "It's probably the lady who thought we were the Water Board."

"You're to go straight up," said the uniformed Sergeant in reception. "Lift to the second floor. Someone will be waiting for you when you get there."

Someone turned out to be a girl with a severe hair style and the sort of look which defied anyone to take liberties with her in business hours. He followed her obediently.

The room they went into was a surprise. It was certainly not the Assistant Commissioner's office. It had more the look of an operations room in an army or air force headquarters. There were two policemen with telephone headsets on. They were seated on high stools in front of a very large plan mounted on a board, and occupying the most of one wall. As far as Petrella could see from where he stood it covered a short length of road and the approaches to some sort of building. It might have been a factory. There were a number of different coloured counters attached to the plan, eight or ten of them were blue, one rather larger one was green and there were three red ones in a row along the bottom. When one of the policemen moved a blue counter, apparently in answer to a telephoned instruction, he saw that they must be magnetised.

There was also a wireless installation, with a loudspeaker, which crackled suddenly and said, "The opposition is arriving. Three small vans, two coming in from the main road on the west. One from the side road on the south-east."

The policeman moved the three red counters into position. The Assistant Commissioner, who was seated in a swivel chair at the head of a long bare table said, "No blue car to move until I give the word. The green can come in now to the main entrance and start normal unloading."

The wireless operator said, "Green move up and unload."

"Blue four, five and six close up gently to Point 'A'."

The men on the board were using both hands now to shift the counters.

It was like the moment in Fighter Command headquarters, thought Petrella, remembering a film he had seen. The moment when all forces were committed.

Two of the three red counters had closed on the green and the other was coming up fast.

"All blue cars move now," said the Assistant Commissioner; "And the best of luck to all concerned."

One of the policemen on the telephone said, "They seem to be putting up a fight, sir."

"Splendid," said the Assistant Commissioner. "I never mind a fight when the odds are three to one in our favour." The policeman grinned. There was a general relaxation of tension. The Assistant Commissioner seemed to notice Petrella for the first time. He said, "I'm afraid you caught us at a busy moment. Come along to my office."

When Samuel reached the front door he took the precaution of looking first through the small viewing glass. A large tweedy lady was standing in front of the door with a sheaf of papers in her hand. She put up her hand and rang the bell again with a touch of impatience. Samuel opened the door and had started to say, "What can I do for you," when the lady placed one of her sensible shoes in the opening to prevent him from closing the door and two men, who had been standing flat against the wall on either side of the door, jumped forward, knocked the door open and surged through.

The Assistant Commissioner said, "That job you were watching was at Warfields, the big building contractors. I expect you know their place out on the M4. It would have been a record haul if they'd got away with it. Warfields have a big Middle-East job on and the money was to pay off the wages of all the English sub-contractors."

Petrella said, "It seemed to go very well, sir."

"Very well indeed. Two of our men were hurt. Four of theirs. Nobody killed. However, that's by the way. What I really wanted to tell you was why I blocked your request for an all stations call and port watch for Adams."

Petrella nearly said, "So it was you who blocked it," but realised, in time, that he was on very thin ice.

"There was no need for anyone to look for Adams. We have him in very safe custody. He's working for us. I don't mean that he's a policeman in disguise. We bought him, three months ago. We had to pay quite highly to secure his allegiance. But I think it was worth it. For instance when he joined us last night he brought with him, from Lloyds' safe, the total proceeds of the Costa-Cans snatch. A lot of it is new notes and some of the other notes have bank markings on them. First-class evidence."

Petrella said, "Yes. I quite see that."

"I've read Superindentent Watterson's report."

Now for it, thought Petrella.

"I'm always telling our people that you can't keep criminal investigation in tidy pigeon holes. This sort of thing is always happening. You approach a matter from one direction. The S.C.S. approach it from another. There's bound to be overlapping. It's the price we pay for specialisation. However, I think we can clear up both ends now. We've not only got Adams's evidence available to us, we've got a very useful statement from Miss Marsh in Liverpool. That's one of the advantages the S.C.S. enjoy. They aren't starved of manpower. They had forty men on the job, at one time and another. All Tillotson girls were under constant supervision. That's how we knew in advance about the Warfields job, of course."

Petrella said, "I suppose both the Masons were involved in it."

"Certainly. They had ten men taking part. We had thirty. Now that the Masons are inside, some of the others will start talking. We may even be able to pin the Nicholls and Lloyd killings on to them. It'll be a long hard fight once the lawyers get going. But I fancy we shall get there in the end."

This seemed to be the cue for Petrella to leave; but the Assistant Commissioner had something else to say. He seemed to be picking his words very carefully.

He said, "I should not have bothered to explain all this to you personally, Inspector, if I had not had a very good report about you from Superintendent Watterson at Division and Commander Baylis at District. You understand?"

"I understand perfectly," said Petrella. "And thank you very much."

As he was walking back across Westminster Bridge he took out two sheets of foolscap paper and tore each of them into sixty-four pieces. Then he threw them over the parapet. A brisk St Valentine's Day breeze caught them and fanned them out and the tiny paper snowflakes floated down and landed on the broad bosom of the Thames.

THE INCREDIBLE ELOPEMENT
OF LORD PETER WIMSEY
by Dorothy L. Sayers

Though her last novel was published over fifty years ago, Dorothy L. Sayers (1893–1957) has remained popular and her work is still widely read. Born and educated in Oxford, she published the first of eleven Lord Peter Wimsey novels, Whose Body?, *in 1923. In addition to the eleven novels, she wrote twenty-one shorter works about Wimsey. All were collected in* Lord Peter *(1972), after the first twenty had previously appeared in earlier collections. She also published a non-Wimsey detective novel, three volumes of mystery short stories, and edited anthologies of mystery and horror stories.*

Sayers eventually turned to writing essays and works with religious themes which included a translation of Dante's Divine Comedy.

"That house, señor?" said the landlord of the little *posada*. "That is the house of the American physician, whose wife, may the blessed saints preserve us, is bewitched." He crossed himself, and so did his wife and daughter.

"Bewitched, is she?" said Langley sympathetically. He was a professor of ethnology, and this was not his first visit to the Pyrenees. He had, however, never before penetrated to any place quite so remote as this tiny hamlet, clinging, like a rockplant, high up the scarred granite shoulders of the mountain. He scented material here for his book on Basque folk-lore. With tact, he might persuade the old man to tell his story.

"And in what manner," he asked, "is the lady bespelled?"

"Who knows?" replied the landlord, shrugging his shoulders. " 'The man that asked questions on Friday was buried on Saturday.' Will your honour consent to take his supper?"

Langley took the hint. To press the question would be to encounter obstinate silence. Later, when they knew him better, perhaps—

His dinner was served to him at the family table— the oily, pepper-flavoured stew to which he was so well accustomed, and the harsh red wine of the country. His hosts chattered to him freely enough in that strange Basque language which has no fellow in the world, and is said by some to be the very speech of our first fathers in Paradise. They spoke of the bad winter, and young Esteban Arramandy, so strong and swift at the pelota, who had been lamed by a falling rock and now halted on two sticks; of three valuable goats carried off by a bear; of the torrential rains that, after a dry summer, had scoured the bare ribs of the mountains. It was raining now, and the wind was howling unpleasantly. This did not trouble Langley; he knew and loved this haunted and impenetrable country at all times and seasons. Sitting in that rude peasant inn, he thought of the oak-panelled hall of his Cambridge college and smiled, and his eyes gleamed happily behind his scholarly pince-nez. He was a young man, in spite of his professorship and the string of letters after his name. To his university colleagues it seemed strange that this man, so trim, so prim, so early old, should spend his vacations eating garlic, and scrambling on mule-back along precipitous mountain-tracks. You would never think it, they said, to look at him.

There was a knock at the door.

"That is Martha," said the wife.

She drew back the latch, letting in a rush of wind and rain which made the candle gutter. A small, aged woman was blown in out of the night, her grey hair straggling in wisps from beneath her shawl.

"Come in, Martha, and rest yourself. It is a bad night. The parcel is ready—oh, yes. Dominique brought it from the town this morning. You must take a cup of wine or milk before you go back."

The old woman thanked her and sat down, panting.

"And how goes all at the house? The doctor is well?"

"He is well."

"And *she*?"

The daughter put the question in a whisper, and the landlord shook his head at her with a frown.

"As always at this time of the year. It is but a month now to the Day of the Dead. Jesu-Maria! it is a grievous affliction for the poor gentleman, but he is patient, patient."

"He is a good man," said Dominique, "and a skilful doctor, but an evil like that is beyond his power to cure. You are not afraid, Martha?"

"Why should I be afraid? The Evil One cannot harm *me*. I have no beauty, no wits, no strength for him to envy. And the Holy Relic will protect me."

Her wrinkled fingers touched something in the bosom of her dress.

"You come from the house yonder?" asked Langley. She eyed him suspiciously.

"The señor is not of our country?"

"The gentleman is a guest, Martha," said the landlord hurriedly. "A learned English gentleman. He knows our country and speaks our language as you hear. He is a great traveller, like the American doctor, your master."

"What is your master's name?" asked Langley. It occurred to him that an American doctor who had buried himself in this remote corner of Europe must have something unusual about him. Perhaps he also was an ethnologist. If so, they might find something in common.

"He is called Wetherall." She pronounced the name several times before he was sure of it.

"Wetherall? Not Standish Wetherall?"

He was filled with extraordinary excitement.

The landlord came to his assistance.

"This parcel is for him," he said. "No doubt the name will be written there."

It was a small package, neatly sealed, bearing the label of a firm of London chemists and addressed to "Standish Wetherall Esq., M.D."

"Good heavens!" exclaimed Langley. "But this is strange. Almost a miracle. I know this man. I knew his wife, too—"

He stopped. Again the company made the sign of the cross.

"Tell me," he said in great agitation, and forgetting his caution, "you say his wife is bewitched—afflicted— how is this? Is she the same woman I know? Describe her. She was tall, beautiful, with gold hair and blue eyes like the Madonna. Is this she?"

There was a silence. The old woman shook her head and muttered something inaudible, but the daughter whispered:

"True—it is true. Once we saw her thus, as the gentleman says—"

"Be quiet," said her father.

"Sir," said Martha, "we are in the hand of God."

She rose, and wrapped her shawl about her.

"One moment," said Langley. He pulled out his note-book and scribbled a few lines. "Will you take this letter to your master the doctor? It is to say that I am here, his friend whom he once knew, and to ask if I may come and visit him. That is all."

"You would not go to that house, excellence?" whispered the old man fearfully.

"If he will not have me, maybe he will come to me here." He added a word or two and drew a piece of money from his pocket. "You will carry my note for me?"

"Willingly, willingly. But the señor will be careful? Perhaps, though a foreigner, you are of the Faith?"

"I am a Christian," said Langley.

This seemed to satisfy her. She took the letter and the money, and secured them, together with the parcel, in a remote pocket. Then she walked to the door, strongly and rapidly for all her bent shoulders and appearance of great age.

Langley remained lost in thought. Nothing could have astonished him more than to meet the name of Standish Wetherall in this place. He had thought that episode finished and done with over three years ago. Of all people! The brilliant surgeon in the prime of his life and reputation, and Alice Wetherall, that delicate piece of golden womanhood—exiled in this forlorn corner of the world! His heart beat a little faster at the thought of seeing her again. Three years ago, he had decided that it would be wiser if he did not see too much of that porcelain loveliness. That folly was past now—but still he could not visualize her except against the background of the great white house in Riverside Drive, with the peacocks and the swimming-pool and the gilded tower with the roof-garden. Wetherall was a rich man, the son of old Hiram Wetherall the automobile magnate. What was Wetherall doing here?

He tried to remember. Hiram Wetherall, he knew, was dead, and all the money belonged to Standish, for there were no other children. There had been trouble when the only son had married a girl without parents or history. He had brought her from "somewhere out west". There had been some story of his having found her, years before, as a neglected orphan, and saved her from something or cured her of something and paid for her education, when he was still scarcely more than a student. Then, when he was a man over forty and she a girl of seventeen, he had brought her home and married her.

And now he had left his house and his money and one of the finest specialist practices in New York to come to live in the Basque country—in a spot so out of the way that men still believed in Black Magic, and could barely splutter more than a few words of bastard French or Spanish—a spot that was uncivilized even by comparison with the primitive civilization surrounding it. Langley began to be sorry that he had written to Wetherall. It might be resented.

The landlord and his wife had gone out to see to their cattle. The daughter sat close to the fire, mending a garment. She did not look at him, but he had the feeling that she would be glad to speak.

"Tell me, child," he said gently, "what is the trouble which afflicts these people who may be friends of mine?"

"Oh!" she glanced up quickly and leaned across to him, her arms stretched out over the sewing in her lap. "Sir, be advised. Do not go up there. No one will stay in that house at this time of the year, except Tomaso, who has not all his wits, and old Martha, who is—"

"What?"

"A saint—or something else," she said hurriedly.

"Child," said Langley again, "this lady when I knew—"

"I will tell you," she said, "but my father must not know. The good doctor brought her here three years ago last June, and then she was as you say. She was beautiful. She laughed and talked in her own speech—for she knew no Spanish or Basque. But on the Night of the Dead—"

She crossed herself.

"All-Hallows Eve," said Langley softly.

"Indeed, I do not know what happened. But she fell into the power of the darkness. She changed. There were terrible cries—I cannot tell. But little by little she became what she is now. Nobody sees her but Martha and she will not talk. But the people say it is not a woman at all that lives there now."

"Mad?" said Langley.

"It is not madness. It is—enchantment. Listen. Two years since on Easter Day—is that my father?"

"No, no."

"The sun had shone and the wind came up from the valley. We heard the blessed church bells all day long. That night there came a knock at the door. My father opened and one stood there like Our Blessed Lady herself, very pale like the image in the church and with a blue cloak over her head. She spoke, but we could not tell what she said. She wept and wrung her hands and pointed down the valley path, and my father went to the stable and saddled the mule. I thought of the flight from bad King Herod. But then—the American doctor came. He had run fast and was out of breath. And she shrieked at sight of him."

A great wave of indignation swept over Langley. If the man was brutal to his wife, something must be done quickly. The girl hurried on.

"He said—Jesus-Maria—he said that his wife was bewitched. At Easter-tide the power of the Evil One was broken and she would try to flee. But as soon as the Holy Season was over, the spell would fall on her again, and therefore it was not safe to let her go. My parents were afraid to have touched the evil thing. They brought out the Holy Water and sprinkled the mule, but the wickedness had entered into the poor beast and she kicked my father so that he was lame for a month. The American took his wife away with him and we never saw her again. Even old Martha does not always see her. But every year the power waxes and wanes—heaviest at Hallow-tide and lifted again at Easter. Do not go to that house, señor, if you value your soul! Hush! they are coming back."

Langley would have liked to ask more, but his host glanced quickly and suspiciously at the girl. Taking up his candle, Langley went to bed. He dreamed of wolves, long, lean and black, running on the scent of blood.

Next day brought an answer to his letter:

Dear Langley, Yes, this is myself, and of course I remember you well. Only too delighted to have you come and cheer our exile. You will find Alice somewhat changed, I fear, but I will explain our misfortunes when we meet. Our household is limited, owing to some kind of superstitious avoidance of the afflicted, but if you will come along about half past seven, we can give you a meal of sorts. Martha will show you the way.

Cordially,

Standish Wetherall

The doctor's house was small and old, stuck halfway up the mountain-side on a kind of ledge in the rock-wall. A stream, unseen but clamorous, fell echoing down close at hand. Langley followed his guide into a dim, square room with a great hearth at one end and, drawn close before the fire, an armchair with wide, sheltering ears. Martha, muttering some sort of apology, hobbled away and left him standing there in the half-light. The flames of the wood fire, leaping and falling, made here a gleam and there a gleam, and, as his eyes grew familiar with the room, he saw that in the centre was a table laid for a meal, and that there were pictures on the walls. One of these struck a familiar note. He went close to it and recognized a portrait of Alice Wetherall that he had last seen in New York. It was painted by Sargent in his happiest mood, and the lovely wildflower face seemed to lean down to him with the sparkling smile of life.

A log suddenly broke and fell in the hearth, flaring. As though the little noise and light had disturbed something, he heard, or thought he heard, a movement from the big chair before the fire. He stepped forward, and then stopped. There was nothing to be seen, but a noise had begun; a kind of low, animal muttering, extremely disagreeable to listen to. It was not made by a dog or a cat, he felt sure. It was a sucking, slobbering sound that affected him in a curiously sickening way. It ended in a series of little grunts or squeals, and then there was silence.

Langley stepped backwards towards the door. He was positive that something was in the room with him that he did not care about meeting. An absurd impulse seized him to run away. He was prevented by the arrival of Martha, carrying a big, old-fashioned lamp, and behind her, Wetherall, who greeted him cheerfully.

The familiar American accents dispelled the atmosphere of discomfort that had been gathering about Langley. He held out a cordial hand.

"Fancy meeting *you* here," said he.

"The world is very small," replied Wetherall. "I am afraid that is a hardy bromide, but I certainly am pleased to see you," he added, with some emphasis.

The old woman had put the lamp on the table, and now asked if she should bring in the dinner. Wetherall replied in the affirmative, using a mixture of Spanish and Basque which she seemed to understand well enough.

"I didn't know you were a Basque scholar," said Langley.

"Oh, one picks it up. These people speak nothing else. But of course Basque is your speciality, isn't it?"

"Oh, yes."

"I daresay they have told you some queer things

about us. But we'll go into that later. I've managed to make the place reasonably comfortable, though I could do with a few more modern conveniences. However, it suits us."

Langley took the opportunity to mumble some sort of inquiry about Mrs Wetherall.

"Alice? Ah, yes, I forgot—you have not seen her yet." Wetherall looked hard at him with a kind of half-smile. "I should have warned you. You were—rather an admirer of my wife in the old days."

"Like everyone else," said Langley.

"No doubt. Nothing specially surprising about it, was there? Here comes dinner. Put it down, Martha, and we will ring when we are ready."

The old woman set down a dish upon the table, which was handsomely furnished with glass and silver, and went out. Wetherall moved over to the fireplace, stepping sideways and keeping his eyes oddly fixed on Langley. Then he addressed the armchair.

"Alice! Get up, my dear, and welcome an old admirer of yours. Come along. You will both enjoy it. Get up."

Something shuffled and whimpered among the cushions. Wetherall stooped, with an air of almost exaggerated courtesy, and lifted it to its feet. A moment, and it faced Langley in the lamplight.

It was dressed in a rich gown of gold satin and lace, that hung rucked and crumpled upon the thick and slouching body. The face was white and puffy, the eyes vacant, the mouth drooled open, with little trickles of saliva running from the loose corners. A dry fringe of rusty hair clung to the halfbald scalp, like the dead wisps on the head of a mummy.

"Come, my love," said Wetherall. "Say how do you do to Mr Langley."

The creature blinked and mouthed out some inhuman sounds. Wetherall put his hand under its forearm, and it slowly extended a lifeless paw.

"There, she recognizes you all right. I thought she would. Shake hands with him, my dear."

With a sensation of nausea, Langley took the inert hand. It was clammy and coarse to the touch and made no attempt to return his pressure. He let it go; it pawed vaguely in the air for a moment and then dropped.

"I was afraid you might be upset," said Wetherall, watching him. "I have grown used to it, of course, and it doesn't affect me as it would an outsider. Not that you are an outsider—anything but that—eh? Premature senility is the lay name for it, I suppose. Shocking, of course, if you haven't met it before. You needn't mind, by the way, what you say. She understands nothing."

"How did it happen?"

"I don't quite know. Came on gradually. I took the best advice, naturally, but there was nothing to be done. So we came here. I didn't care about facing things at home where everybody knew us. And I didn't like the idea of a sanatorium. Alice is my wife, you know—sickness or health, for better, for worse, and all that. Come along; dinner's getting cold."

He advanced to the table, leading his wife, whose dim eyes seemed to brighten a little at the sight of food.

"Sit down, my dear, and eat your nice dinner. (She understands that, you see.) You'll excuse her table-manners, won't you? They're not pretty, but you'll get used to them."

He tied a napkin around the neck of the creature and placed food before her in a deep bowl. She snatched at it hungrily, slavering and gobbling as she scooped it up in her fingers and smeared face and hands with the gravy.

Wetherall drew out a chair for his guest opposite to

where his wife sat. The sight of her held Langley with a kind of disgusted fascination.

The food—a sort of salmis—was deliciously cooked, but Langley had no appetite. The whole thing was an outrage, to the pitiful woman and to himself. Her seat was directly beneath the Sargent portrait, and his eyes went helplessly from the one to the other.

"Yes," said Wetherall, following his glance. "There is a difference, isn't there?" He himself was eating heartily and apparently enjoying his dinner. "Nature plays sad tricks upon us."

"Is it always like this?"

"No; this is one of her bad days. At times she will be—almost human. Of course these people here don't know what to think of it all. They have their own explanation of a very simple medical phenomenon."

"Is there any hope of recovery?"

"I'm afraid not—not of a permanent cure. You are not eating anything."

"I—well, Wetherall, this has been a shock to me."

"Of course. Try a glass of burgundy. I ought not to have asked you to come, but the idea of talking to an educated fellow-creature once again tempted me, I must confess."

"It must be terrible for you."

"I have become resigned. Ah, naughty, naughty!" The idiot had flung half the contents of her bowl upon the table. Wetherall patiently remedied the disaster, and went on:

"I can bear it better here, in this wild place where everything seems possible and nothing unnatural. My people are all dead, so there was nothing to prevent me from doing as I liked about it."

"No. What about your property in the States?"

"Oh, I run over from time to time to keep on eye

on things. In fact, I am due to sail next month. I'm glad you caught me. Nobody over there knows how we're fixed, of course. They just know we're living in Europe."

"Did you consult no American doctor?"

"No. We were in Paris when the first symptoms declared themselves. That was shortly after that visit you paid to us." A flash of some emotion to which Langley could not put a name made the doctor's eyes for a moment sinister. "The best men on this side confirmed my own diagnosis. So we came here."

He rang for Martha, who removed the salmis and put on a kind of sweet pudding.

"Martha is my right hand," observed Wetherall. "I don't know what we shall do without her. When I am away, she looks after Alice like a mother. Not that there's much one can do for her, except to keep her fed and warm and clean—and the last is something of a task."

There was a note in his voice which jarred on Langley. Wetherall noticed his recoil and said:

"I won't disguise from you that it gets on my nerves sometimes. But it can't be helped. Tell me about yourself. What have you been doing lately?"

Langley replied with as much vivacity as he could assume, and they talked of indifferent subjects till the deplorable being which had once been Alice Wetherall began to mumble and whine fretfully and scramble down from her chair.

"She's cold," said Wetherall. "Go back to the fire, my dear."

He propelled her briskly towards the hearth, and she sank back into the armchair, crouching and complaining and thrusting out her hands towards the blaze. Wetherall brought out brandy and a box of cigars.

"I contrive just to keep in touch with the world, you see," he said. "They send me these from London. And

I get the latest medical journals and reports. I'm writing a book, you know, on my own subject; so I don't vegetate. I can experiment, too—plenty of room for a laboratory, and no Vivisection Acts to bother one. It's a good country to work in. Are you staying here long?"

"I think not very."

"Oh! If you had thought of stopping on, I would have offered you the use of this house while I was away. You would find it more comfortable than the *posada,* and I should have no qualms, you know, about leaving you alone in the place with my wife—under the peculiar circumstances."

He stressed the last words and laughed. Langley hardly knew what to say.

"Really, Wetherall—"

"Though, in the old days, *you* might have liked the prospect more and *I* might have liked it less. There was a time, I think, Langley, when you would have jumped at the idea of living alone with—*my wife.*"

Langley jumped up.

"What the devil are you insinuating, Wetherall?"

"Nothing, nothing. I was just thinking of the afternoon when you and she wandered away at a picnic and got lost. You remember? Yes, I thought you would."

"This is monstrous," retorted Langley. "How dare you say such things—with that poor soul sitting there—?"

"Yes, poor soul. You're a poor thing to look at now, aren't you, my kitten?"

He turned suddenly to the woman. Something in his abrupt gesture seemed to frighten her, and she shrank away from him.

"You devil!" cried Langley. "She's afraid of you. What have you been doing to her? How did she get into this state? I *will* know!"

"Gently," said Wetherall. "I can allow for your natural agitation at finding her like this, but I can't have you coming between me and *my wife*. What a faithful fellow you are, Langley. I believe you still want her—just as you did before when you thought I was dumb and blind. Come now, have you got designs on *my wife*, Langley? Would you like to kiss her, caress her, take her to bed with you—my beautiful wife?"

A scarlet fury blinded Langley. He dashed an inexpert fist at the mocking face. Wetherall gripped his arm, but he broke away. Panic seized him. He fled stumbling against the furniture and rushed out. As he went he heard Wetherall very softly laughing.

The train to Paris was crowded. Langley, scrambling in at the last moment, found himself condemned to the corridor. He sat down on a suitcase and tried to think. He had not been able to collect his thoughts on his wild flight. Even now, he was not quite sure what he had fled from. He buried his head in his hands.

"Excuse me," said a polite voice.

Langley looked up. A fair man in a grey suit was looking down at him through a monocle.

"Fearfully sorry to disturb you," went on the fair man. "I'm just tryin' to barge back to my jolly old kennel. Ghastly crowd, isn't it? Don't know when I've disliked my fellow-creatures more. I say, you don't look frightfully fit. Wouldn't you be better on something more comfortable?"

Langley explained that he had not been able to get a seat. The fair man eyed his haggard and unshaven countenance for a moment and then said:

"Well, look here, why not come and lay yourself down in my bin for a bit? Have you had any grub? No? That's a mistake. Toddle along with me and we'll get hold of a spot of soup and so on. You'll excuse my mentioning it, but you look as if you'd been backing a system that's come unstuck, or something. Not my business, of course, but do have something to eat."

Langley was too faint and sick to protest. He stumbled obediently along the corridor till he was pushed into a first-class sleeper, where a rigidly correct manservant was laying out a pair of mauve silk pyjamas and a set of silver-mounted brushes.

"This gentleman's feeling rotten, Bunter," said the man with the monocle, "so I've brought him in to rest his aching head upon thy breast. Get hold of the commissariat and tell 'em to buzz a plate of soup along and a bottle of something drinkable."

"Very good, my lord."

Langley dropped, exhausted, on the bed, but when the food appeared he ate and drank greedily. He could not remember when he had last made a meal.

"I say," he said, "I wanted that. It's awfully decent of you. I'm sorry to appear so stupid. I've had a bit of a shock."

"Tell me all," said the stranger pleasantly.

The man did not look particularly intelligent, but he seemed friendly and, above all, normal. Langley wondered how the story would sound.

"I'm an absolute stranger to you." he began.

"And I to you," said the fair man. "The chief use of strangers is to tell things to. Don't you agree?"

"I'd like—" said Langley. "The fact is, I've run away from something. It's queer—it's—but what's the use of bothering you with it?"

The fair man sat down beside him and laid a slim hand on his arm.

"Just a moment," he said. "Don't tell me anything

if you'd rather not. But my name is Wimsey—Lord Peter Wimsey—and I am interested in queer things."

It was the middle of November when the strange man came to the village. Thin, pale, and silent, with his great black hood flapping about his face, he was surrounded with an atmosphere of mystery from the start. He settled down, not at the inn, but in a dilapidated cottage high up in the mountains, and he brought with him five mule-loads of mysterious baggage and a servant. The servant was almost as uncanny as the master; he was a Spaniard and spoke Basque well enough to act as an interpreter for his employer when necessary; but his words were few, his aspect gloomy and stern, and such brief information as he vouchsafed, disquieting in the extreme. His master, he said, was a wise man; he spent all his time reading books; he ate no flesh; he was of no known country; he spoke the language of the Apostles and had talked with blessed Lazarus after his return from the grave; and when he sat alone in his chamber by night, the angels of God came and conversed with him in celestial harmonies.

This was terrifying news. The few dozen villagers avoided the little cottage, especially at night-time; and when the pale stranger was seen coming down the mountain path, folded in his black robe and bearing one of his magic tomes beneath his arm, the women pushed their children within doors, and made the sign of the cross.

Nevertheless, it was a child that first made the personal acquaintance of the magician. The small son of the Widow Etcheverry, a child of bold and inquisitive disposition, went one evening adventuring into the unhallowed neighbourhood. He was missing for two hours, during which his mother, in a frenzy of anxiety, had called the neighbours about her and summoned the priest, who had unhappily been called away on business to the town. Suddenly, however, the child reappeared, well and cheerful, with a strange story to tell.

He had crept up close to the magician's house (the bold, wicked child, did ever you hear the like?) and climbed into a tree to spy upon the stranger (Jesu-Maria!). And he saw a light in the window, and strange shapes moving about and shadows going to and fro within the room. And then there came a strain of music so ravishing it drew the very heart out of his body, as though all the stars were singing together. (Oh, my precious treasure! The wizard has stolen the heart out of him, alas! alas!) Then the cottage door opened and the wizard came out and with him a great company of familiar spirits. One of them had wings like a seraph and talked in an unknown tongue, and another was like a wee man, no higher than your knee, with a black face and a white beard, and he sat on the wizard's shoulder and whispered in his ear. And the heavenly music played louder and louder. And the wizard had a pale flame all about his head, like the pictures of the saints. (Blessed St James of Compostella, be merciful to us all! And what then?) Why then he, the boy, had been very much frightened and wished he had not come, but the little dwarf spirit had seen him and jumped into the tree after him, climbing—oh! so fast! And he had tried to climb higher and had slipped and fallen to the ground. (Oh, the poor, wicked, brave, bad boy!)

Then the wizard had come and picked him up and spoken strange words to him and all the pain had gone away from the places where he had bumped himself (Marvellous! marvellous!) and he had carried him into the house. And inside, it was like the streets of Heaven, all gold and glittering. And the familiar spirits had sat beside the fire, nine in number, and the music had stopped playing. But the wizard's servant had brought him marvellous fruits in a silver dish, like fruits of Paradise, very sweet and delicious, and he had eaten them, and drunk a strange, rich drink from a goblet covered with red and blue jewels. Oh, yes—and there had been a tall crucifix on the wall, big, big, with a lamp burning before it and a strange sweet perfume like the smell in church on Easter Day.

(A crucifix? That was strange. Perhaps the magician was not so wicked, after all. And what next?)

Next, the wizard's servant had told him not to be afraid, and had asked his name and his age and whether he could repeat his Paternoster. So he had said that prayer and the Ave Maria and part of the Credo, but the Credo was long and he had forgotten what came after *"ascendit in coelum"*. So the wizard had prompted him and they had finished saying it together. And the wizard had pronounced the sacred names and words without flinching and in the right order, so far as he could tell. And then the servant had asked further about himself and his family, and he had told about the death of the black goat and about his sister's lover, who had left her because she had not so much money as the merchant's daughter. Then the wizard and his servant had spoken together and laughed, and the servant had said: "My master gives this message to your sister: that where there is no love there is no wealth, but he that is bold shall have gold for the asking." And with that, the wizard had put forth his hand into the air and taken from it—out of the empty air, yes, truly—one, two, three, four, five pieces of money and given them to him. And he was afraid to take them till he had made the sign of the cross upon them, and then, as they did not vanish or turn into fiery serpents, he had taken them, and here they were!

So the gold pieces were examined and admired in

fear and trembling, and then, by grandfather's advice, placed under the feet of the image of Our Lady, after a sprinkling with Holy Water for their better purification. And on the next morning, as they were still there, they were shown to the priest, who arrived, tardy and flustered upon his last night's summons, and by him pronounced to be good Spanish coin, whereof one piece being devoted to the Church to put all right with Heaven, the rest might be put to secular uses without peril to the soul. After which, the good padre made his hasty way to the cottage, and returned, after an hour, filled with good reports of the wizard.

"For, my children," said he, "this is no evil sorcerer, but a Christian man, speaking the language of the Faith. He and I have conversed together with edification. Moreover, he keeps very good wine and is altogether a very worthy person. Nor did I perceive any familiar spirits or flaming apparitions; but it is true that there is a crucifix and also a very handsome Testament with pictures in gold and colour. *Benedicite,* my children. This is a good and learned man."

And away he went back to his presbytery; and that winter the chapel of Our Lady had a new altar-cloth.

After that, each night saw a little group of people clustered at a safe distance to hear the music which poured out from the wizard's windows, and from time to time a few bold spirits would creep up close enough to peer through the chinks of the shutters and glimpse the marvels within.

The wizard had been in residence about a month, and sat one night after his evening meal in conversation with his servant. The black hood was pushed back from his head, disclosing a sleek poll of fair hair, and a pair of rather humorous grey eyes, with a cynical droop of the lids. A glass of Cockburn 1908 stood on the table at his elbow and from the arm of his chair a red-and-green parrot gazed unwinkingly at the fire.

"Time is getting on, Juan," said the magician. "This business is very good fun and all that—but is there anything doing with the old lady?"

"I think so, my lord. I have dropped a word or two here and there of marvellous cures and miracles. I think she will come. Perhaps even tonight."

"Thank goodness! I want to get the thing over before Wetherall comes back, or we may find ourselves in Queer Street. It will take some weeks, you know, before we are ready to move, even if the scheme works at all. Damn it, what's that?"

Juan rose and went into the inner room, to return in a minute carrying the lemur.

"Micky had been playing with your hair-brushes," he said indulgently, "Naughty one, be quiet! Are you ready for a little practice, my lord?"

"Oh, rather, yes! I'm getting quite a dab at this job. If all else fails, I shall try for an engagement with Maskelyn."

Juan laughed, showing his white teeth. He brought out a set of billiard-balls, coins, and other conjuring apparatus, palming and multiplying them negligently as he went. The other took them from him, and the lesson proceeded.

"Hush!" said the wizard, retrieving a ball which had tiresomely slipped from his fingers in the very act of vanishing. "There's somebody coming up the path."

He pulled his robe about his face and slipped silently into the inner room. Juan grinned, removed the decanter and glasses and extinguished the lamp. In the firelight the great eyes of the lemur gleamed strongly as it hung on the back of the high chair. Juan pulled a large folio from the shelf, lit a scented pastille in a curiously shaped copper vase, and pulled forward a heavy iron cauldron which stood on the hearth. As he piled the logs about it, there came a knock. He opened the door, the lemur running at his heels.

"Whom do you seek, mother?" he asked, in Basque.

"Is the Wise One at home?"

"His body is at home, mother; his spirit holds converse with the unseen. Enter. What would you with us?"

"I have come, as I said—ah, Mary! is that a spirit?"

"God made spirits and bodies also. Enter and fear not."

The old woman came tremblingly forward.

"Hast thou spoken with him of what I told thee?"

"I have. I have shown him the sickness of thy mistress—her husband's sufferings—all."

"What said he?"

"Nothing; he read in his book."

"Think you he can heal her?"

"I do not know; the enchantment is a strong one; but my master is mighty for good."

"Will he see me?"

"I will ask him. Remain here, and beware thou show no fear, whatever befall."

"I will be courageous," said the old woman, fingering her beads.

Juan withdrew. There was a nerve-shattering interval. The lemur had climbed up to the back of the chair again and swung, teeth-chattering, among the leaping shadows. The parrot cocked his head and spoke a few gruff words from his corner. An aromatic steam began to rise from the cauldron. Then, slowly into the red light, three, four, seven white shapes came stealthily and sat down in a circle about the hearth. Then, a faint music, that seemed to roll in from leagues away. The flame flickered and dropped. There was a tall cabinet against the wall, with gold figures on it that seemed to move with the moving firelight.

Then, out of the darkness, a strange voice chanted in an unearthly tongue that sobbed and thundered.

Martha's knees gave under her. She sank down. The seven white cats rose and stretched themselves, and came sidling slowly about her. She looked up and saw the wizard standing before her, a book in one hand and a silver wand in the other. The upper part of his face was hidden, but she saw his pale lips move and presently he spoke, in a deep, husky tone that vibrated solemnly in the dim room:

'ὦ πέπον, εἰ μὲν γὰρ, πόλεμον περὶ τόνδε φυγόντε,
αἰεὶ δὴ μέλλοιμεν ἀγήρω τ' ἀθανάτω τε
ἔσσεθ', οὔτε κεν αὐτὸς ἐνὶ πρώτοισι μαχοίμην,
οὔτε κέ σε στέλλοιμι μάχην ἐς κυδιάνειραν . . .''

The great syllables went rolling on. Then the wizard paused and added, in a kinder tone:

"Great stuff, this Homer. 'It goes so thunderingly as though it conjured devils.' What do I do next?"

The servant had come back, and now whispered in Martha's ear.

"Speak now," said he. "The master is willing to help you."

Thus encouraged, Martha stammered out her request. She had come to ask the Wise Man to help her mistress, who lay under an enchantment. She had brought an offering—the best she could find, for she had not liked to take anything of her master's during his absence. But here were a silver penny, an oat-cake, and a bottle of wine, very much at the wizard's service, if such small matters could please him.

The wizard, setting aside his book, gravely accepted the silver penny, turned it magically into six gold pieces and laid the offering on the table. Over the oat-cake and the wine he showed a little hesitation, but at length, murmuring:

> *"Ergo omnis longo solvit se Teucria luctu"*

(a line notorious for its grave spondaic cadence), he metamorphosed the one into a pair of pigeons and the other into a curious little crystal tree in a metal pot, and set them beside the coins. Martha's eyes nearly started from her head, but Juan whispered encouragingly:

"The good intention gives value to the gift. The master is pleased. Hush!"

The music ceased on a loud chord. The wizard, speaking now with greater assurance, delivered himself with fair accuracy of a page or so from Homer's Catalogue of the Ships, and, drawing from the folds of his robe his long white hand laden with antique rings, produced from mid-air a small casket of shining metal, which he proffered to the suppliant.

"The master says," prompted the servant, "that you shall take this casket, and give to your lady of the wafers which it contains, one at every meal. When all have been consumed, seek this place again. And remember to say three Aves and two Paters morning and evening for the intention of the lady's health. Thus, by faith and diligence, the cure may be accomplished."

Martha received the casket with trembling hands.

"Tendebantque manus ripae ulterioris amore," said the wizard, with emphasis. *"Poluphloisboio thalasses. Ne plus ultra. Valete. Plaudite."*

He stalked away into the darkness, and the audience was over.

"It is working, then?" said the wizard to Juan.

The time was five weeks later, and five more consignments of enchanted wafers had been ceremoniously dispatched to the grim house on the mountain.

"It is working," agreed Juan. "The intelligence is returning, the body is becoming livelier, and the hair is growing again."

"Thank the Lord! It was a shot in the dark, Juan, and even now I can hardly believe that anyone in the world could think of such a devilish trick. When does Wetherall return?"

"In three weeks' time."

"Then we had better fix our grand finale for today fortnight. See that the mules are ready, and go down to the town and get a message off to the yacht."

"Yes, my lord."

"That will give you a week to get clear with the menagerie and the baggage. And—I say, how about Martha? Is it dangerous to leave her behind, do you think?"

"I will try to persuade her to come back with us."

"Do. I should hate anything unpleasant to happen to her. The man's a criminal lunatic. Oh, lord! I'll be glad when this is over. I want to get into a proper suit of clothes again. What Bunter would say if he saw this—"

The wizard laughed, lit a cigar, and turned on the gramophone.

The last act was duly staged a fortnight later.

It had taken some trouble to persuade Martha of the necessity of bringing her mistress to the wizard's house. Indeed, that supernatural personage had been obliged to make an alarming display of wrath and declaim two whole choruses from Euripides before gaining his point. The final touch was put to the terrors of the evening by a demonstration of the ghastly effects of a sodium flame—which lends a very corpselike aspect to the human countenance, particularly in a lonely cottage on a dark night, and accompanied by incantations and the *Danse Macabre* of Saint-Saens.

Eventually the wizard was placated by a promise, and Martha departed, bearing with her a charm, engrossed upon parchment, which her mistress was to read and thereafter hang about her neck in a white silk bag.

Considered as a magical formula, the document was perhaps a little unimpressive in its language, but its meaning was such as a child could understand. It was in English, and ran:

> You have been ill and in trouble, but your friends are ready to cure you and help you. Don't be afraid, but do whatever Martha tells you, and you will soon be quite well and happy again.

"And even if she can't understand it," said the wizard to his man, "it can't possibly do any harm."

The events of that terrible night have become legend in the village. They tell by the fireside with bated breath how Martha brought the strange, foreign lady to the wizard's house, that she might be finally and for ever freed from the power of the Evil One. It was a dark night and a stormy one, with the wind howling terribly through the mountains.

The lady had become much better and brighter through the wizard's magic—though this, perhaps, was only a fresh glamour and delusion—and she had followed Martha like a little child on that strange and secret journey. They had crept out very quietly to elude the vigilance of old Tomaso, who had strict orders from the doctor never to let the lady stir one step from the house. As for that, Tomaso swore that he had been cast into an enchanted sleep—but who knows? There may have been no more to it than over-much wine. Martha was a cunning woman, and, some said, little better than a witch herself.

Be that as it might, Martha and the lady had come to the cottage, and there the wizard had spoken many things in a strange tongue, and the lady had spoken likewise. Yes—she who for so long had only grunted like a beast, had talked with the wizard and answered him. Then the wizard had drawn strange signs upon the floor round about the lady and himself. And when the lamp was extinguished, the signs glowed awfully, with a pale light of their own. The wizard also drew a circle about Martha herself, and warned her to keep inside it. Presently they heard a rushing noise, like great wings beating, and all the familiars leaped about, and the little white man with the black face ran up the curtain and swung from the pole. Then a voice cried out: "He comes! He comes!" and the wizard opened the door of the tall cabinet with gold images upon it, that stood in the centre of the circle, and he and the lady stepped inside it and shut the doors after them.

The rushing sound grew louder and the familiar spirits screamed and chattered—and then, all of a sudden, there was a thunder-clap and a great flash of light and the cabinet was shivered into pieces and fell down. And lo and behold! the wizard and the lady had vanished clean away and were never more seen or heard of.

This was Martha's story, told the next day to her neighbours. How she had escaped from the terrible house she could not remember. But when, some time after, a group of villagers summoned up courage to visit the place again, they found it bare and empty. Lady, wizard, servant, familiars, furniture, bags, and baggage—all were gone, leaving not a trace behind them, except a few mysterious lines and figures traced on the floor of the cottage.

This was a wonder indeed. More awful still was the disappearance of Martha herself, which took place three nights afterwards.

Next day, the American doctor returned, to find an empty hearth and a legend.

"Yacht ahoy!"

Langley peered anxiously over the rail of the *Abracadabra* as the boat loomed out of the blackness. When the first passenger came aboard, he ran hastily to greet him.

"Is it all right, Wimsey?"

"Absolutely all right. She's a bit bewildered, of course—but you needn't be afraid. She's like a child, but she's getting better every day. Bear up, old man—there's nothing to shock you about her."

Langley moved hesitatingly forward as a muffled female figure was hoisted gently on board.

"Speak to her," said Wimsey. "She may or may not recognize you. I can't say."

Langley summoned up his courage. "Good evening, Mrs Wetherall," he said, and held out his hand.

The woman pushed the cloak from her face. Her blue eyes gazed shyly at him in the lamplight—then a smile broke out upon her lips.

"Why, I know you—of course I know you. You're Mr Langley. I'm so glad to see you."

She clasped his hand in hers.

"Well, Langley," said Lord Peter, as he manipulated the syphon, "a more abominable crime it has never been my fortune to discover. My religious beliefs are a little ill-defined, but I hope something really beastly happens to Wetherall in the next world. Say when!

"You know, there were one or two very queer points

about that story you told me. They gave me a line on the thing from the start.

"To begin with, there was this extraordinary kind of decay or imbecility settlin' in on a girl in her twenties—so conveniently, too, just after you'd been hangin' round the Wetherall home and showin' perhaps a trifle too much sensibility, don't you see? And then there was this tale of the conditions clearin' up regularly once a year or so—not like any ordinary brain-trouble. Looked as if it was being controlled by somebody.

"Then there was the fact that Mrs Wetherall had been under her husband's medical eye from the beginning, with no family or friends who knew anything about her to keep a check on the fellow. Then there was the determined isolation of her in a place where no doctor could see her and where, even if she had a lucid interval, there wasn't a soul who could understand or be understood by her. Queer, too, that it should be a part of the world where you, with your interests, might reasonably be expected to turn up some day and be treated to a sight of what she had turned into. Then there were Wetherall's well-known researches, and the fact that he kept in touch with a chemist in London.

"All that gave me a theory, but I had to test it before I could be sure I was right. Wetherall was going to America, and that gave me a chance; but of course he left strict orders that nobody should get into or out of his house during his absence. I had, somehow, to establish an authority greater than his over old Martha, who is a faithful soul, God bless her! Hence, exit Lord Peter Wimsey and enter the magician. The treatment was tried and proved successful—hence the elopement and the rescue.

"Well, now, listen—and don't go off the deep end. It's all over now. Alice Wetherall is one of those unfor-

tunate people who suffer from congenital thyroid deficiency. You know the thyroid gland in your throat—the
one that stokes the engine and keeps the old brain going.
In some people the thing doesn't work properly, and
they turn out cretinous imbeciles. Their bodies don't
grow and their minds don't work. But feed 'em the stuff,
and they come absolutely all right—cheery and handsome and intelligent and lively as crickets. Only, don't
you see, you have to *keep* feeding it to 'em, otherwise
they just go back to an imbecile condition.

"Wetherall found this girl when he was a bright young
student just learning about the thyroid. Twenty years
ago, very few experiments had been made in this kind of
treatment, but he was a bit of a pioneer. He gets hold
of the kid, works a miraculous cure, and bein' naturally
bucked with himself, adopts her, gets her educated, likes
the look of her, and finally marries her. You understand,
don't you, that there's nothing fundamentally unsound
about those thyroid deficients. Keep 'em going on the
little daily dose, and they're normal in every way, fit to
live an ordinary life and have ordinary healthy children.

"Nobody, naturally, knew anything about this thyroid business except the girl herself and her husband. All
goes well till *you* come along. Then Wetherall gets
jealous—"

"He had no cause."

Wimsey shrugged his shoulders.

"Possibly, my lad, the lady displayed a preference—
we needn't go into that. Anyhow, Wetherall did get jealous and saw a perfectly marvellous revenge in his power.
He carried his wife off to the Pyrenees, isolated her from
all help, and then simply sat back and starved her of her
thyroid extract. No doubt he told her what he was going
to do, and why. It would please him to hear her desperate

appeals—to let her feel herself slipping back day by day, hour by hour, into something less than a beast—"

"Oh, God!"

"As you say. Of course, after a time, a few months, she would cease to know what was happening to her. He would still have the satisfaction of watching her—seeing her skin thicken, her body coarsen, her hair fall out, her eyes grow vacant, her speech die away into mere animal noises, her brain go to mush, her habits—"

"Stop it, Wimsey."

"Well, you saw it all yourself. But that wouldn't be enough for him. So, every so often, he would feed her the thyroid again and bring her back sufficiently to realize her own degradation—"

"If only I had the brute here!"

"Just as well you haven't. Well then, one day—by a stroke of luck—Mr Langley, the amorous Mr Langley, actually turns up. What a triumph to let him see—"

Langley stopped him again.

"Right-ho! but it was ingenious, wasn't it? So simple. The more I think of it, the more it fascinates me. But it was just that extra refinement of cruelty that defeated him. Because, when you told me the story, I couldn't help recognizing the symptoms of thyroid deficiency, and I thought, "Just supposing"—so I hunted up the chemist whose name you saw on the parcel, and, after unwinding a lot of red tape, got him to admit that he had several times sent Wetherall consignments of thyroid extract. So then I was almost sure, don't you see.

"I got a doctor's advice and a supply of gland extract, hired a tame Spanish conjurer and some performing cats and things, and barged off complete with disguise and a trick cabinet devised by the ingenious Mr Devant. I'm a bit of a conjurer myself, and between us we didn't do so badly. The local superstitions helped, of course, and so did the gramophone records. Schubert's "Unfinished" is first class for producing an atmosphere of gloom and mystery, so are luminous paint and the remnants of a classical education."

"Look here, Wimsey, will she get all right again?"

"Right as ninepence, and I imagine that any American court would give her a divorce on the grounds of persistent cruelty. After that—it's up to you!"

Lord Peter's friends greeted his reappearance in London with mild surprise.

"And what have *you* been doing with yourself?" demanded the Hon. Freddy Arbuthnot.

"Eloping with another man's wife," replied his lordship. "But only," he hastened to add, "in a purely Pickwickian sense. Nothing in it for yours truly. Oh, well! Let's toddle round to the Holborn Empire, and see what George Robey can do for us."